CURSED CITY

E.COOMBE

THE CURSED CITY

A Lothian Children's Book

Published in Australia and New Zealand in 2013
by Hachette Australia
(an imprint of Hachette Australia Pty Limited)
Level 17, 207 Kent Street, Sydney NSW 2000
www.hachettechildrens.com.au

10 9 8 7 6 5 4 3 2

National Library of Australia
Cataloguing-in-Publication data:

Coombe, E.

The cursed city / E. Coombe
Arky Steele 2

978 0 7344 1160 0 (pbk.)

A823.4

Cover design by Xou Creative
Text design by Bookhouse, Sydney
Typeset in 12.75/19 pt Garamond Premier Pro
Printed and bound in Australia by McPherson's Printing Group

MIX
Paper from
responsible sources
FSC® C001695

The paper this book is printed on is certified against the
Forest Stewardship Council® Standards. McPherson's Printing
Group holds FSC® chain of custody certification SA-COC-005379.
FSC® promotes environmentally responsible, socially beneficial
and economically viable management of the world's forests.

For Bowie

Prologue

Extract from the journal of Alfonso Pezaro, a conquistador, written in the year 1550.

After being wounded in a battle with the Aztecs, Francisco and I became lost in the jungle, succumbed to fever and collapsed.

We awoke many days later, weak and dismayed to find ourselves in a concealed city with a strange people who worshipped us as gods. We were given fine food and taught their language, but kept prisoner in the king's palace.

King Huemac ruled this city. He worshipped his mummified ancestor who lay nearby, encrusted with jade, in a golden room. King Huemac believed his ancestor demanded human sacrifice so he could live again and fly to the gods.

On the first day of the new moon, we were taken to a ceremony atop a stone pyramid beneath a terrifying volcano. There, an evil sorcerer, wearing a cloak of human skin, cut out the hearts of hundreds of people with an obsidian knife.

Shortly after this awful ritual, people began to die of the speckled fever. The sorcerer blamed us for the disease and demanded the king put us to death, saying we were not gods. We wanted to escape but the ever-watching eyes of our guards prevented us and the way out of the valley was hidden.

The king refused to have us killed but, eventually, he too sickened. We were taken to his bedside and ordered to cure him. While we were there, the king died. The sorcerer rushed us with his knife. We fought and mortally wounded him but he cursed us with his last breath.

We took his knife and precious jade box of secrets. Francisco opened the box, rifled through the sorcerer's fetishes, and pulled out a drawing, showing the secrets to the city.

Using this drawing, we fled, but Francisco suddenly weakened. By the time we reached the jungle my friend moved no more. Fearing the sorcerer's curse, I placed Francisco's body in care of a jaguar and let a monster swallow the jade box. I left the sorcerer's dagger to open the way.

I crossed a snake river and spent days lumbering through a swamp. I climbed a terrible ravine, where fever took me. I have no memory of how I was rescued.

A Walk to the Waterfall

'I can't believe my dad's going off to hunt for a lost Toltec city and leaving us out of it!' Arky angrily kicked a stone on the steep jungle track. 'And he's not coming with us to visit the Aztec ruins like he promised.'

'My stepfather's paying for Doc to go exploring, but I'm not included like I was last time,' Bear huffed, his face going red in the tropical heat. 'It's like I don't count at all!'

'I think you count,' Arky replied, stopping for a moment to check Bear was okay. Arky's disappointment about being left out of an adventure with Doc weighed like a stone in his gut. But if he felt bad, he knew his best friend must be devastated.

Bear had been in boarding school since their adventure together in Asia several months ago. Lord Wright, Bear's stepfather, had paid for Arky and Bear to go with Doc on a trip to Mongolia. Many disasters had befallen them, but to everyone's surprise they had discovered Genghis Khan's lost tomb, his crown, the infamous Hand of Death and loads of treasure.

Their adventure had made them friends, so when Bear was sent to boarding school they kept in touch and chatted on their computers.

Arky knew Bear was very excited about being in Central America. Every time he had talked to Bear they had swapped information about Aztecs and their ancient stone cities. Arky even knew that the Aztecs had fought huge battles with the Toltecs. The Toltecs were a race of people who had similar beliefs to the Aztecs. They had mysteriously vanished, taking hoards of treasure with them.

'Even your mum was surprised Doc's not coming on our holiday.' Bear sounded frustrated. 'I bet she's wondering why we had to come all the way to this sacred Aztec well just to be told Doc has a big expedition planned. He could have told her on the phone and saved us the trouble of driving out here!'

'I guess he didn't want to talk on the phone,' Arky whispered. 'Dad said he has to keep his discovery of the Spanish Diary secret. He said the diary talked about a mummified king encrusted with gold and jade. You and I both know that Rulec's probably having my dad and your stepfather watched. If we suddenly changed our holiday plans and disappeared into the wilds, he'd figure out we were up to something.'

'Rulec!' Bear scowled. The cold-eyed billionaire had tried to kill Arky and Bear in Mongolia, and he'd also stolen Genghis Khan's crown and the golden Hand of Death.

'He'd try to steal the Jade-encrusted King if he knew about it.' Arky walked faster along the track, trying not to think about Goran Rulec. He was a rich and powerful enemy of Bear's stepfather, Lord Wright. If Rulec discovered the news about Doc's

Spanish Diary and the quest for a lost ancient city, he'd stop at nothing to get there first.

'I guess you're right,' Bear reasoned. 'I wonder if Rulec has spies out. What about the woman your dad hired to do the cooking and cleaning up at the camp?'

Arky thought about Camilla, the lady who was working at the camp. She had a beautiful smile and nothing was too much trouble for her. She even picked up Bear's clothes and tidied the tents. Arky almost forgave her for having Mia with her. Her little daughter was pretty annoying. 'Camilla speaks good English, so she might be able to pick up some gossip. But I can't see her working for Rulec. Besides, I think Dad's kept the news about finding the Spanish Diary very secret. He hasn't said anything about it in front of Camilla or Mia.'

Bear groaned. 'Mia followed me around all yesterday afternoon wanting to play baseball.'

Arky laughed. 'She's taken a bit of a shine to you! Doc and Pancho are packing everything up today and we're all leaving tomorrow, so we'll be rid of her then.'

Bear grimaced. 'I only agreed to go on this stupid walk to get away from her!

Arky wiped the sweat out of his eyes. 'You know, last night when Dad was telling us about the Spanish Diary and the clues in it that might lead to a lost city, I thought he was going to ask us to come with him. I was really shocked when he said we couldn't come.'

'Maybe he doesn't think your mum would let us go,' suggested Bear. 'Maybe they're discussing it now, which is why they told us to go for a walk and find this waterfall. You know how grown-ups always talk about stuff out of our hearing.'

Arky thought about Bear's suggestion. 'It can't be just Rulec that Dad's worried about. We coped with him last time and he knows we're good at being out in wild places. Maybe you're right—it's Mum who doesn't want us to go. Mum would rather climb mountains than go hunting for a lost city in a jungle. She knows we nearly got killed in Mongolia so I don't think she'd want us to go.'

'Pancho is going.' Bear's green eyes flashed jealousy. 'What do you think of him?'

Arky thought about the man searching for relics in the sacred Aztec waterhole with his father. At first Arky had been amused by Pancho's enormous moustache. The monster whiskers covered half of his chubby cheeks, hid his mouth and wiggled hilariously when he talked. Sometimes food got stuck in the hairs. Arky couldn't watch him eat. 'I don't mind him,' Arky replied, 'but I think Dad was a bit disappointed. Dad was expecting a doctor of archaeology to come up here to help him recover artefacts, but he got Pancho instead.'

'Pancho said he's studying to become an archaeologist. I guess your dad thought it would be good experience for him to go on the expedition instead of us,' Bear said.

'He's a good diver and he loves finding artefacts.' Arky remembered how Pancho had enthusiastically shown the boys the jade and gold relics he had discovered in the depths of the Sacred Well. Pancho had also explained how the Aztecs had thrown the treasures into the waters as offerings to the water gods. 'Maybe the lost city is underwater.'

'Doc's putting a team together and going into the jungle and there's no room for us,' Bear wailed again, not letting go of his disappointment. 'Pancho will be there instead of us when they find the jade-encrusted mummy and a whole city. I can't get over it!'

'The city might not exist and they may just wander around in the heat.' A large blue butterfly flitted in front of Arky's eyes and he waved it away.

'I wish we could read the Spanish Diary,' Bear said. 'Even Pancho hasn't been allowed to see it.'

'Dad said he scanned it into his computer and it's locked in a hotel safe back in town,' Arky grumbled. 'We'll never get the chance to see it.'

'Is that the waterfall I hear?' interrupted Bear, stopping to listen. The tropical heat was obviously getting to him: his face was as red as a beetroot. 'Race you to it.' He took off down the track and Arky had to run hard to catch him.

The path led them to the promised waterfall which tumbled into a pool. 'Woo hoo, but I'm hot.' Bear eyed the water.

'Doc told us not to swim and asked us to come straight back for breakfast,' Arky reminded Bear.

'A few seconds to cool off won't hurt.' Bear smiled, ignoring Arky's objection and peeling off his clothes. 'It looks deep,' he added, jumping naked into the water and emerging in a burst of bubbles.

Bear's smile was so broad that Arky knew the water must be lovely and cool. He threw caution and his clothes away and leapt in after his best friend. 'It's great!' He laughed, surfacing.

'Beat you to the other side,' Bear said, striking out. Bear was no sportsman, so he always stole the head start. Arky, light and wiry, kicked out after him. He swam hard and caught Bear in seconds. They both touched the opposite bank at the same time.

'Tie!' Bear laughed. 'Beat you back to our clothes!' This time, Arky won easily.

'Get out!' called a voice. A small girl with long dark plaits, wearing a long skirt and white shirt, stood on the track beside the pool, waving her hands furiously. 'Get out!' she shrieked.

'Mia followed us,' Arky whispered. He shouted at her. 'We're not playing baseball. Just go away! Leave us alone.'

'Bad! Bad to have no clothes!' screeched Mia.

'Then go away and don't look.' Arky splashed water at Mia. 'Go back to your mother.'

'No. Bad! Candiru, candiru! Danger, candiru!'

'Kangaroo?' puzzled Bear. 'She thinks there are kangaroos?'

'This is Central America,' yelled Arky, splashing water at her again. 'There are no kangaroos. Go away!'

'No, not kangaroo. CANDIRU! A feesh. It sweem up your weelly.'

'A feesh?' asked Bear, mystified. 'It sweem up your wheelie?'

'Fish,' suggested Arky, 'and it swims up your . . .' He paled.

'Good grief!' yelped Bear, grabbing his privates.

Mia politely turned her back as the boys shot from the pool.

Standing in the sun, Arky and Bear frantically checked themselves for anything unusual. 'I seem okay,' said Bear, the colour coming back to his face. 'Was she taking the piss?'

'No,' replied Mia, her back still turned. 'I not go to the toilet.'

'He means, are you teasing us?' snapped Arky.

'I not teasing. I see you swim,' Mia replied. 'I see danger. The candiru, he looks like a little toothpick. He swims up people. He eats blood. He kills animals and people.'

'That's why Doc told us not to swim,' Arky grouched, pulling on his pants. 'Couldn't he just have told us about the fish?'

'Are you dressed now?' Mia asked. 'Can I turn?'

'Yes,' replied Bear, still pale from his fright, as he pulled on his shirt. 'How do you know if the fish has swum up you?'

'If it swims up, it hurts, but it's too late then,' Mia informed them as she turned. 'Many bad things in the jungle.'

'That's totally ruined my day.' Bear shuddered, looking back at the pool. 'I just don't believe it!'

'We'll check she's not having us on when we get back,' Arky said. 'But I suspect she's telling the truth.'

'*She* is beside you!' Mia said indignantly. 'I have a name. I tell the truth! I not go to heaven if I lie.'

Arky shrugged and, ignoring her, he and Bear began walking back to the campsite beside the Sacred Well.

Danger at the Sacred Well

Arky led Bear and Mia back along the waterfall track. They stopped to get their breath at a rocky outcrop that gave them a clear view down through the trees to their campsite. The Sacred Well glimmered sapphire blue in the morning sunlight, a bright contrast against the heavy green jungle.

Their tents were erected in a clearing, serviced by a rough, rutted bush road. A truck was parked beside the mess tent. Camilla, Mia's mother, was preparing the breakfast dishes. Her bright red bandana and long heavy skirt were different from the blue jeans and yellow shirt Alice, Arky's mum, wore.

Alice, her long dark hair shining in the sunlight, was carrying wrapped artefacts to a large packing box. Pancho and Doc stood behind the truck sorting their diving gear and getting ready to pack up and leave. Doc's slightly stooped, well-muscled body made him appear small compared to Pancho's massive shoulders and strong chest.

'My mother is sad you are going,' Mia said. 'This is the only job she gets.'

'Where's your father?' Arky asked.

'Dead.' Mia didn't seem too concerned. 'When I was a baby.'

'Is your village far?' Arky asked, but he was watching the activity below.

'Many hours' drive in your truck. Pancho will take us home later today. I will not see you tomorrow. Can you play baseball with me before you go?'

Arky nodded. 'We'll play this afternoon. Once the work is done.'

'Who's that?' said Bear, pointing. A bare-chested man with long braided hair suddenly emerged from the dense forest near the campsite below, carrying a large machete.

Mia gave a cry of fear. 'Suarez!' She ducked behind a tree. 'Hide! Hide!'

Before the boys could ask why she was so frightened, three men carrying guns erupted from the trees behind the newcomer. A shot reverberated through the air. Pancho dropped what he was doing, spun around and, seeing the invaders, held up his hands. Doc ducked behind the truck, but a fifth man emerged from the trees almost beside him, gun levelled. Doc was captured in an instant.

Alice, seeing the bandits, turned and ran towards the jungle, but another shot rang out. Arky's heart raced hard as a bullet raised the earth near her feet. Camilla screamed and Alice stopped in her tracks. She turned to see Suarez holding his machete against Camilla's throat. Suarez beckoned Alice to return and stand beside Camilla.

Arky wanted to race down and free his parents but Bear had pulled him down behind some bushes. Mia was white with fear.

Once they had their hostages under control, Suarez made the women unpack the box of artefacts. He held each item up for inspection. The jade and gold treasures seemed to cheer him, and a few of them made him slap his thigh with pleasure. Then he passed the best ones around to his men for inspection.

'How do you know this Suarez?' Bear asked Mia, keeping low behind the bushes, but not taking his eyes from the terrible scene below.

'They came to our village,' Mia said. 'Our church had many old paintings and golden icons. Then one day, my mother and I were cleaning the church. This was my mother's job. Suarez came with bandits. He made us lie down. He shot the priest in the leg and stole everything. Now our village is poor. There are no jobs. No tourists come to see the paintings. Our priest had to go to hospital and never came back.'

Once the artefacts had been checked, Suarez ordered his bandits to go through the tents, looking for phones and other valuable possessions. They made a pile of phones, put them in bags and tossed them into the Sacred Well. Then Pancho and Doc were ordered to take down the tents.

'They are going to steal everything!' Bear said as the prisoners dismantled the campsite.

Arky noticed that his parents and Camilla never looked around for him, Bear or Mia. He knew the adults would be hoping they had heard the shots and had the sense to stay hidden.

'The bandits don't know we're here,' he said. 'They're not looking for us.'

'What can we do?' Bear asked.

'Watch and wait.' Arky kept an eye on Suarez. 'Our parents would be more worried if we were captured.'

Suarez made the women repack the artefacts and load them into the truck. Then the bandits filled the truck with tents, tables, chairs, suitcases and anything useful.

When the truck was jam-packed, one of the bandits squeezed into the driver's seat and drove the laden vehicle away.

Suarez and the other bandits pointed their guns at the hostages and marched them into the forest.

'He's taking them!' cried Arky, horrified to see Alice and Doc disappearing into the trees. 'Where's he taking them? Why?'

'Your family is rich,' Mia said to Bear, her voice shaking. 'Everyone knows that. I think it is for ransom.'

'Then why take your mother and Pancho?' Bear asked, but his voice rose in fear.

'If the ransom is not paid, they shoot my mother first to show they mean the business.' Mia sobbed. 'And Pancho is studying at a university so he must be rich too. They will get a ransom for him.'

Arky felt sick. 'We have to do something!'

'We can go and get help,' Bear suggested.

'It's a day's drive to the nearest village!' Arky yelled. 'The trip up here was just forest and more forest. It'd take us forever to walk out!'

'These bad men hide in the jungle so the police can't find them,' Mia said quietly. 'We must follow and find their hiding place. Then we save my mother.'

'Where did the truck go then?' Bear asked.

'I think the truck will go somewhere like a barn, and they will hide the treasures. Then they sell them bit by bit, so no one knows where they came from.

But our parents, they will be hidden in the jungle away from a road. Somewhere hard to find.'

'What if Rulec found out about the Spanish Diary?' Arky asked. 'What if he's behind this and wants Dad's computer?'

'If he got the diary, then he might not let them go,' Bear said, his voice on the edge of panic. 'He's tried to kill us before. Maybe he'll get this bandit to hold them hostage and get the information out of them.'

'Mia's right. We have to follow,' Arky said, standing up from behind the bushes. 'We have to save our parents.'

Jungle Horrors

After the sound of Suarez's machete hacking at the jungle had faded, the children crept down into the deserted camp. A broken chair lay against a tree, plastic bags flapped in a light breeze and several food items lay scattered in the dirt.

Arky remembered that Doc and Pancho had stowed some gear down by the Sacred Well. He raced to see if anything was still there, and was rewarded with their backpack, a first aid kit and a knife.

Back at the camp, Bear and Mia rescued a crushed packet of biscuits, a squeeze-bottle full of honey, several tins of fruit and an open packet of tortillas. Bear also found a small plastic sachet with Spanish writing on the label. It looked like raspberry jam so he put it in his pocket.

Arky found two little candles and a lighter. Mia found a tin-opener, a plastic plate, two spoons and some empty plastic bottles. Arky took the bottles and started to head for the well to fill them with water.

'Rainwater only!' Mia yelled out.

Arky sighed. 'We'll need water,' he said. 'It's so hot in the jungle and it's still only morning.'

'Fruit from the tins only,' Mia insisted. 'The well water makes you poo.'

Arky nodded, realising that Mia was most likely right, and threw the bottles away.

When their meagre supplies were packed, Arky shouldered the backpack and the trio headed towards the forbidding jungle. Because Arky had read books his teacher had lent him about Central America's wildlife, he worried about how they would cope with biting insects and wild animals. Their clothes and shoes were not designed for a jungle trek. And what chance did they have with a little girl in tow? Arky also wished he had a plan. What would they do, even if they did find their parents? He sighed loudly. 'They've got about a half-hour's head start,' he said. 'Mia, you will have to keep up. We can't afford for you to slow us down'.

Mia's dark eyes flashed with annoyance. 'I live here. I can keep up with you!' She tucked her skirt into her undies and strode out after them.

For a while they made good time following the bandits' trail, looking for places where the machete had hewn down a branch or cut away bushes. Towards noon, the jungle opened out and there were no more machete cuts, so they had to search the ground, looking for footprints.

'I'm tired and hot and the jungle is awful and we'll never find them,' Bear grumbled as he searched. He continued complaining and Arky smiled, knowing his friend was quick to grumble but usually meant well.

Mia, however, was not so happy with Bear. She strode up to him and poked him in the chest. 'You are a big scaredy-cat!'

'I'm not!' Bear huffed, blushing at her assault.

Arky was about to stop her from saying anything else when he noticed something glittering at her feet.

'Stop arguing and look,' he shouted, diving on a silver coin, gleaming in the leaf litter. 'Someone's leaving clues. Keep your eyes open and work together.'

The find refocused them and they moved on, Bear discovering another coin and then Mia, a button from a shirt.

'I think the hostages are leaving a trail,' Arky said, as he noticed a bent stick then a scratch on a tree.

By afternoon, tired and hot, Arky called a halt. Mia had tears in her eyes so Arky smiled warmly at her and offered her the first share of biscuits from the pack. Bear opened up a tin of fruit. Arky slurped down his ration and noticed Bear was looking at Mia with what looked like deep respect. He had to admit he admired her too. Not only had she stopped Bear's habit of grumbling, she was strong and had kept up with Arky and Bear, and *she* hadn't complained once.

But then Arky realised that Bear was staring at Mia with a strange intensity. Something was wrong.

Arky directed his gaze at Mia, almost jumping in horror. A large black slimy lump was growing behind her ear.

Mia noticed their gaze. 'What?' she asked.

Arky didn't want to frighten her. 'Do you know what is black and slimy and might hang off people's skin?' he asked, trying to broach the subject delicately.

'You found it then?' Mia smiled, and stared at Bear. 'I didn't want Bear to scream.'

'What is it?' Bear was amazed that Mia could be so brave. 'Does it kill you?'

Mia shook her head. 'No, it only sucks your blood. It is a leech. You should not worry, Bear. I can pull the one on the back of your neck off.'

'Back of *my* neck?' Bear squealed, leaping to his feet and slapping at his neck. His fingers found the hideous worm and he let out a yelp and shuddered. Mia calmly reached over, pulled the leech off and stomped it into the ground. There was a sickening pop as the blood-laden creature burst.

Blood trickled down the back of Bear's neck.

Dismayed by the flow, he paled and clamped his hand over the wound. Blood ran down his arm.

'The leech put something in your blood that makes it run for a long time,' Mia explained. 'You'll be all right soon. Just looks bad.'

'Mia, you have one behind your ear,' Arky said, feeling a bit sick.

'Me?' Mia said. 'Why didn't you say so?' She lifted her hand, found the leech, gritted her teeth and pulled hard. The leech flew from her fingers into the bush and her neck ran red, staining her white shirt.

'It looks like vampires have had a go at you both.' Arky shuddered.

'Vampires come at night,' Mia said, in a matter-of-fact voice. 'We are wasting time. We must move.'

'She's my hero,' Bear whispered as Mia marched behind them.

The jungle trail became steep and slippery with mud. Terrible prickle bushes tore at Arky's clothes, and Bear's arms were scratched. But the bushes also made it easier to follow a trail of machete chops and remnants of the hostages' clothing.

In the heat of the jungle, sweat poured from Arky's body. He could see Mia and Bear were suffering too. He knew they had to keep their fluids up. He made the other two stop and he opened the last of the fruit tins. While they sucked down the juice, Arky studied Bear's concerned face. He could see Mia was worried about her mother too. *I hope we haven't made a terrible mistake coming into the jungle,* he thought. *If we don't find our parents, how will we find our way back to camp?* 'We better press on,' he said, trying to look cheerful.

Late in the afternoon, Bear found Camilla's red bandana hanging on a tree. Then their hearts leapt with hope; they could hear a song playing on a radio. Someone was nearby. They crept forward warily, until they spied a clearing with two huts and a large rainwater tank. They'd found the bandits.

Attacked

Arky counted four armed men. Two were on the verandah of the hut closest to them, playing cards and listening to the radio. A third bandit was cooking over a blazing fire beside the verandah. And the fourth sat propped against the door of the second hut with a gun resting on his lap. The second hut was further away and had strong walls, a metal roof, and no windows. It looked like a prison. A heavy door behind the guard had three sliding bolts on the outside. Suarez was nowhere to be seen.

Arky was relieved they had finally found where their parents were being held. He gestured to Bear and Mia to lie flat on the ground and they all kept watch.

The smell of food cooking and the sight of the water tank made Arky feel even more hungry and thirsty. He undid the backpack and handed everyone a tortilla from the packet. They chewed the cornbread slowly and watched.

A little while later, Bear remembered the little sachet in his pocket. He was sure the small amount of sweetness and moisture from the jam would help him swallow what was left of the tortilla. As there was not enough to share around, he secretly opened the packet and squeezed the contents onto the last bit of his tortilla. He rolled up the bread and squished it into his mouth, swallowing it whole so the others didn't see.

It took a second for him to taste the jam. It burned his tongue and throat. A red-hot fire filled his nasal passages. His face flushed and his eyes ran with water. It wasn't jam—it was chilli paste! The heat brought a sob to his throat.

'Now what?' Arky whispered, his eyes focused on his parents' prison.

'Nothing!' choked Bear, then realised that Arky hadn't seen his misery and was just asking what they should do next. 'I can't think of anything,' he managed to splutter.

'I've no idea either.' Arky was watching the bandit cook put four bowls on a tray and take them to the prison hut. The guard unbolted the door and Doc appeared. He wasn't chained or shackled. He took the bowls from the cook and handed them inside. The prison door was then slammed in his face and re-bolted.

Bear realised the chilli paste was creating havoc in his guts and making terrible gas. Unable to control the build-up, he farted so loudly that Arky and Mia nearly jumped out of their skin.

One of the bandit card players picked up his gun and stood up. Bear was terrified his fart had given them away. To his relief, the bandit walked over to the prison and changed places with the guard at the door.

'Go back into the jungle, stinky boy,' Mia whispered.

'Good idea,' Arky said. 'Somewhere we can't hear you.'

Embarrassed, Bear did as he was asked.

❖

Later, still watching the clearing, Arky began twitching and wriggling.

'What's wrong?' Mia asked.

'There's something under my pants,' Arky whispered. Suddenly a painful bite, then another, made him leap to his feet. He gritted his teeth so he didn't yell, dashed behind a large tree and dropped his trousers.

On his leg were two brown ants with spanner-like jaws gripping his thigh and tearing at his flesh. Arky tried to prise one away. It hung on. He pulled hard. The ant's body ripped away but its head remained firmly stuck to his skin.

'They're eating holes in me,' he moaned when Mia and Bear joined him.

'I think you've got army ants on you.' Bear knelt down and inspected the insects. 'I read about them. They send scouts out to look for food. The scouts then produce some sort of chemical message, and millions of them come and eat anything dead, lying down or sleeping. Apparently they can devour a whole cow in hours.'

'We were lying down,' Arky said, trying to pull the other ant off, with the same lack of success. 'I must have collected some scouts.'

'There's more over there,' Mia said, pointing to a nearby bush writhing with hundreds of ants. The bush seemed to grow bigger and bigger as more ants swarmed from the jungle and others scuffled in Arky's direction.

'The ants on your leg might have marked you with a scent,' Bear said, jumping back and farting. Arky tripped over his pants as the ants raced towards him. He was down on the ground and vulnerable. He didn't want another one of those painful bites, or to be devoured like a cow! He managed to get up and shuffled sideways fast, pulling up his pants. The ants turned, following him.

Arky zigzagged around some trees. The ants also zigged and zagged.

'They're following you!' Bear sounded panicked. Arky managed to remove his backpack, get out the first aid kit and open a strong disinfectant. He also found some tweezers. He raced ahead of the following ant swarm and quickly pulled his pants down again. He yanked off the ants' heads and disinfected the wounds. 'No scent now,' he said, hitching his pants and putting the pack on. He darted away from the invading army.

The scurrying insects followed him. As he moved, they moved.

'Why won't they let me go?' he asked, feeling scared.

'Maybe they smell something on you,' Mia suggested. 'The food perhaps?'

'Good idea.' Bear wrenched the backpack from Arky. Instantly, the ants forgot Arky and moved towards Bear.

Arky noticed a stain on the bottom of the pack. He moved closer and touched it. His fingers came away sticky. He sniffed. 'Honey!' he cried. 'The squeeze-bottle's leaking.'

'We'll toss it away,' Bear said, hurriedly opening the pack.

'Did you say they ate sleeping things?' Arky asked, now very worried. 'It's getting dark. We have to sleep sometime. Even if we give them the honey they'll find us later.'

'The honey would distract them for a bit,' Bear replied, pulling the bottle out.

'We mustn't sleep,' Mia said. 'We could move to the other side of the clearing, away from the bandits.'

'Bandits . . . ?' Arky had an idea. 'Bandits have to sleep.'

Bear watched the bandits while Arky and Mia moved around the jungle in slow circles, keeping the ants busy until it was almost too dark to see. Luckily there was a full moon, so some filtered light helped them.

Finally, Bear reported that the lights had gone off in the bandits' hut. 'They must be asleep. Only the guard is awake. He has a lantern beside him and he's reading.'

'Are you ready?' Mia's voice was shaking in anticipation.

'Indeed I am,' Arky replied, dribbling a little honey onto the soles of his shoes. Then, holding the squeeze-bottle, he headed towards the clearing. The full moon was a problem now, as the guard might see him, but he couldn't afford to wait. With his heart hammering in fear, he made his way slowly out of the jungle, creeping as silently as possible towards the back of the sleeping bandits' hut.

He could barely believe it when he reached the shadow of the hut without the guard noticing. Loud snores issued from a partially open window. Arky squeezed honey on the ground under the window and up the walls. Then he poured the last of it onto the sill, letting it dribble inside. He propped the squeeze-bottle against the hut and stood back.

A shadowy ripple travelled across the clearing behind him. Thousands of ants, following the honeyed trail, marched past Arky, swarmed up the walls and disappeared through the window. Minutes later, the snoring was replaced with squeals of pain—and then terror.

The guard outside the prison was instantly alerted. He dropped his book, grabbed his lantern and ran to help his amigos. Simultaneously, Bear dashed from the jungle to the unguarded prison and began unbolting the door.

Arky's parents had no doubt been roused by the agonised screams of the bandits. When Bear managed to open the door, they were waiting inside tensely. They looked amazed as Bear stood before them, silvered in the moonlight, and let off a trumpet of terrified farts.

They stumbled outside, and Bear re-bolted the prison door behind them. He pointed to a tiny light, flickering in the jungle, and ran towards it with the adults following.

Mia had done her job well. She had lit one of the candles so she could be found easily. She had walked slowly amongst the trees. Even if one of the bandits had looked into the jungle at that moment, they would have thought the tiny moving light was a darting firefly.

When Arky joined them all, Mia blew out her candle. Doc and Alice hugged Arky so hard he almost lost his breath. Camilla scooped Mia into her arms.

'I can't believe you found us,' Alice cried, giving Bear a kiss. 'We left clues in case you managed to show the police where we went, but we never thought you'd follow yourselves.'

Pancho shook Arky's hands over and over again. 'You are very brave!' he exclaimed. He shook Bear's and Mia's hands too. 'All of you!'

Back at the huts there were screams and shrieks of agony. The four bandits were so involved in their battle with the ants they hadn't noticed their prisoners had escaped.

'We'd better get a move on,' Doc said, as the bandits burst out of their hut. One tripped down the verandah steps and rolled on the ground, beating at the ants covering his body. The others leapt and screamed around the campsite. In the clear moonlight, a shadowy column of ants poured down the steps after them. Finally the bandits took off across the clearing, running for their lives. They reached the rainwater tank, climbed up and jumped into the water.

Luck at Last

Once they left the bandits' camp behind them, Doc and Alice took charge of the group, and they headed blindly into the jungle, trying to put as much distance as possible between them and the bandits. The jungle quickly blotted out the moonlight and they crashed into bushes and tripped over roots while branches whipped their faces. Animals scuttled in the bushes and monkeys made screeching noises in the trees.

'Where are we going?' Arky asked, worried they would get lost. 'We'll never be able to retrace our steps like this.'

'We can't do that anyway,' Pancho replied. 'Once those bandits get out of the water, they'll realise we're missing and assume we will try to return the way we came. They'll go that way first!'

As the night wore on, and there was no sign they were being followed, Arky started to feel a little safer, but he was very tired. To his dismay, Mia was still going strong. He gritted his teeth. If she could keep going, then he could keep moving too.

Eventually, they stumbled across a cleared track. Moonlight lit the trail so they could finally see where they were going. The find lifted everyone's spirits and they picked up their pace, but they walked in silence so they could hear if anyone was coming behind them. Bear didn't even grumble, although Arky could tell he was tired. As a pre-dawn light created a little colour in the surrounding leaves, the team almost stumbled into the back of a farmhouse.

'We should be careful,' Pancho warned, as a rooster crowed. 'We are not far from our kidnappers. The people who live here could be their friends. Stay hidden. I'll go and scout out who is here.' He left the jungle, and disappeared around the front of the house, returning minutes later. His face was grim.

'It is very bad luck,' he whispered. 'It is the bandits' house. We should get away as fast as possible.'

'Are you sure?' Doc sounded disappointed.

'Our truck is parked out the front, still fully packed,' Pancho said. 'We will have to go back into the jungle. It is too dangerous.'

'I don't think we can.' Alice glanced at Mia, who was clinging to her mother's legs. Arky's eyes had black rings of exhaustion under them. 'We have no food or water and the children need rest.'

'You won't believe this,' Doc said, reaching into his trouser pocket, 'but I've got a spare key to the truck. And it is very, *very* early in the morning so everyone should still be asleep.'

With Pancho leading the way, they crept around the house to the truck. Bear nearly tripped over a rusty piece of metal but Arky kept him upright. Doc and Pancho carefully opened the truck's passenger door and pulled out some of the tightly packed gear to make room for the four adults and three children.

They worked as fast as possible. Arky kept looking back at the house, terrified someone would wake inside and spot them.

Finally, there was enough room. Arky and Bear wriggled in behind the driver's seat and squashed themselves together. Arky was too tired and frightened to complain that Bear's bottom was inches from his face. Pancho pushed in beside him, and Alice and Camilla squeezed into the passenger seat, nursing Mia.

Doc took the driver's seat and put the keys into the ignition. Arky held his breath. Great tears of tension rolled down Mia's face. Doc fired up the truck and gunned the engine. The wheels spun and the truck bounced forward. As they tore down the drive, Doc looked in the rear-view mirror.

Suarez, naked and hairy, clutching a rifle, threw open the farmhouse door and bolted outside. He raised the gun and fired at the truck. Doc swerved. The truck swayed dangerously but the bullets missed. Suarez fired a second volley as the truck rounded a corner.

Doc drove like a crazy man towards safety. Amidst the bumps and bucking of the truck, and Bear's smelly bottom, Arky fell asleep.

❖

As the truck vanished down the jungle road, Suarez swore mightily and fired several more shots in anger. Behind him, several sleepy men appeared.

'You may be the boss, but we left you on watch!' a small man with a big beard said.

'You missed,' grumbled a man with a scar on his forehead. 'Your aim was bad! We have lost everything.'

Suarez swung his gun and aimed it at the scar-faced man. 'Shut up!' he roared. 'I won't miss you!' He glared at the other men. 'How did they escape? How did they start the truck? They better have killed their guards because, if not, I'm going to!' He turned and strode towards the bandits, pushing them roughly out of the way. 'You are all incompetent! Where are your guns? Why weren't you shooting?'

He stormed back inside the house, picked up his mobile phone and punched in a number. He couldn't let his men see how humiliated he was that his prisoners had not just escaped, but found his hideout, taken back their artefacts, and made him a laughing stock.

'We have lost our guests,' he said to the person on the other end. 'They haven't paid their bill. Not only that . . . they have stolen something that is mine.'

'They will come to me then,' replied a voice. 'I will find out what is happening and let you know.'

'I want them punished and what is mine returned,' insisted Suarez. 'I want you to earn your money this time.'

Spies at Work

Lieutenant Gatto of the Guatemalan police stared in amazement at the three brave children. He couldn't believe a slight, blue-eyed boy called Archibald Steele and a rich boy called Belvedere Elron Apollo Redford had rescued four hostages from the notorious bandit Suarez the Slaughterer. As for the little girl, Mia, he shook his head in disbelief.

He turned to his assistant, Corporal Topi, a brooding man with a neatly trimmed beard. 'Organise a police escort to the city museum and make sure the artefacts are delivered safely,' he ordered. 'Then we will begin a manhunt in the area described by Doctor Lukas Steele and Pancho Alverez to see if we can find Suarez.'

Corporal Topi twisted a large gold ring on his finger. 'A police escort for the truck?' he said. 'Is that necessary? One man could drive it there safely.'

'An escort is needed!' Gatto's craggy face showed deep concern. 'We have been embarrassed by Suarez before. I don't want it to happen again.'

'As you order.' Topi looked slightly annoyed. 'And our visitors, do they need an escort?' He turned and flashed a wide smile at Alice and Camilla. 'I understand you are all staying at the Palace Hotel?'

'We are,' said Alice. 'But the boys and I are planning to fly out in three days' time to go to Mexico. If you capture these men, will we have to come back for a trial?'

'Sadly, I doubt we will find them.' Lieutenant Gatto rubbed his grey hair in a gesture of frustration. 'We have hunted Suarez for years. The thieves in our country are getting bolder all the time. Suarez's gang of bandits is growing and he seems to have many contacts. He also has a successful business taking wealthy people hostage. You are not his first victims. If I were you, I'd be very careful. Don't leave your hotel. Suarez has a nasty habit of getting revenge if he is thwarted.'

'Alice and the boys will leave for Mexico as planned,' Doc said. 'But Pancho and I have more work to do in the jungle.'

'Yes.' Pancho smiled, his big moustache bristling with anticipation. 'We will be continuing with our work.'

'You should really leave with your family, Doctor Steele,' Inspector Gatto said. 'It will be dangerous for you here.'

'We have a small exploration organised,' Doc replied. 'Pancho has a team ready to go in a few days' time.'

Arky tried not to look too glum at the thought of the treasures his father and Pancho might find.

'And where is this trip?' Gatto asked. 'And what is it you are looking for?'

'I can't say where we're going exactly,' Doc said, leaning closer, 'but it is in a remote region. I think there could be a lost city. I can bring you the government permissions for our expedition but, because of the nature of our trip, I'm afraid I can say no more about it at the moment.'

'Then I will expect you back at the police station so I can see your permission.' Gatto reached into his pocket and handed everyone his card. 'If anyone has any trouble or suspicions, please ring me—day or night. Now, I think we'll organise some cars.' He smiled at the children. 'I suspect these young folk would like a shower and a good meal!'

'You bet,' said Bear, 'and a swim in the pool.'

'I have never been in a hotel,' Mia said. 'It sounds wonderful.'

Shortly after everyone was settled into the hotel, Corporal Topi made a phone call.

'They are at the Palace. I couldn't get to the truck. Gatto had it guarded. It was never left alone.' Topi winced as Suarez yelled abuse at him. 'Well, there is a manhunt out for you,' he snapped. Then, almost mockingly, he added, 'And your hostages were freed by three little kids.' Topi held the phone away from his ear for several seconds until Suarez calmed down.

'There is something you should know, and I want my cut for this information.' Topi kept his voice low. 'One of those kids has very, *very* rich parents: Lord Wright, the billionaire, and Linda Redford, the film actress. They'd pay to get him back. Also, the archaeologists are searching for a lost city. It must be something particularly good or they'd be getting out of here after their experience with you. I suspect Doctor Steele has information stored in his hotel safe. Maybe you could kill two birds with one stone. Get the kid and crack the safe to get the information. You could retire on this one.' Topi smiled this time as Suarez spoke. 'So, you are in town. Then I'd not show your face—every policeman is after you. Send someone else to the hotel. They've put on extra security and they'll need to be dealt with too. I'll meet you this afternoon and explain which kid to grab.'

❖

A little while later, Goran Rulec, the longtime enemy of Bear's stepfather, Lord Wright, received an international phone call.

Rulec had answered the phone in his private museum inside his mansion in Europe. His hard eyes darkened as he listened to the voice of his spy in Central America. 'What do you mean you haven't got the Spanish Diary?' he said. 'I know Doctor Steele has it on his computer and I have gone to a lot of trouble to put you in a position to get it.'

Rulec began pacing up and down amongst his precious treasures. 'You say a band of ignorant cut-throats are ruining our plan?' Rulec stopped beside a golden mirror and straightened his tie as his informant gave him more news. 'So, you think Suarez will go after them in revenge. Then you must get the computer with the Spanish Diary from Doctor Steele today.' Rulec glared at a precious vase as the caller started complaining. 'Get one of your gang to do it then, if you're afraid. It can't be that hard. Do it! I want the Jade-encrusted King. If you fail, I will make sure the authorities find out about your other enterprises.'

Attacked

Later that day, after everyone had settled into their hotel rooms, Doc, Alice, Camilla and Pancho went to the hotel rooftop restaurant to have a coffee, while Bear and Arky decided they would like a swim in the pool.

'You know,' said Bear, while changing into his bathers in their bedroom, 'I'd like to see that diary. What if we sneaked a look?'

'I'd like to, but we really shouldn't,' Arky said.

'But it would be amazing to read it and at least know where Doc's going!' Bear gave Arky a cheeky look—he knew Arky loved archaeology and history.

Arky shook his head.

Bear sighed. 'I suppose the computer is locked away so you couldn't possibly get to it, even if you wanted.'

'I could if I wanted,' Arky said quickly.

Bear's eyes glinted with mischief. 'What harm would it be if we just looked?' he argued. 'We'd only be a minute and we'd put it straight back. Doc would never know.' Bear opened the door that connected their hotel bedroom to Doc and Alice's room.

'We shouldn't,' Arky said again, but he followed Bear into his parents' room.

Bear smiled, knowing curiosity had got the better of Arky's nature.

Once in front of the hotel safe, Arky guiltily punched Doc's birthday into the combination lock and opened the door. He pulled out the laptop, turned it on and keyed in Doc's password.

It didn't take long to find the file they were looking for. 'It's in Spanish,' Arky moaned. 'We wasted our time.'

'Copy it and open up a Spanish–English translation site,' Bear said. 'You paste it in and it automatically translates.'

Very soon the boys had read the translated words of the dead conquistador, Pezaro.

'I don't know how you could find a city based on this,' Bear said, sounding disappointed. 'There are no clues at all.'

'There are clues,' Arky said. 'Pezaro mentions a volcano, a river, a swamp and a big ravine. If I was my dad I'd look for those things on a map. They'd have to be close together as Pezaro couldn't walk too far if he was sick.'

'Look!' Bear took the computer from Arky and returned to Doc's file. 'You're right. Your dad's put together a map. Let's check it against your clues.'

The boys began studying the map and comparing it to the diary translation.

'Pezaro talks of a volcano beside the lost city,' Arky said, reading the diary again and looking closer at the map. 'And there's a volcano here. Then Pezaro says he crossed a snake river. The river on Dad's map is windy like a snake.'

'But Pezaro could have meant it was full of snakes,' Bear said. 'Doc could be wrong.'

'But there is a swamp near this ravine.' Arky pointed to the map. 'So, you could put all those clues together and say you were on the right track. The city has to be near that volcano.'

'Where exactly?' Bear opened up a bigger map of the area from the internet.

'It looks like the river flows from a mountain range and is surrounded by thick jungle, about two hundred kilometres from here.' Arky sighed. 'It's such a shame we can't go.'

'Here are some notes Doc's written,' Bear said, opening another document. 'The jade-encrusted mummy was once called King Huemac. He was a Toltec king who hid himself away from the Aztecs. He fought with the Aztecs and sacrificed all his prisoners by cutting their hearts out or skinning them!'

'Horrible!' Arky didn't want to think about it.

'Worse,' Bear said. 'He had a sorcerer who made him kill his own children and he had other children sacrificed on mountain tops!' He read silently for a moment. 'King Huemac finally killed himself. He hanged himself in his hidden city, but his son, another King Huemac, covered him in jade and gold and worshipped his body. He made the people believe the first King Huemac wasn't dead but a sleeping god. He would wake one day and everyone would see him fly . . .'

The boys were so absorbed in the gruesome story that they didn't hear the hotel door being unlocked and opened behind them.

Arky was alerted by a moving reflection in the computer screen. Thinking Doc had caught them, his heart jumped a guilty beat. He looked up to apologise and a heavy-set man with four fingers on one hand grabbed Bear and the computer from behind.

As the man hooked Bear off his feet and pinned him under one arm, Bear instinctively hugged the computer to his chest. He yelled and kicked like a maniac, but he couldn't get away at all. The man was too strong.

Arky launched himself at the man, beating him with his fists. He felt like his hands were hitting a brick wall. The man pushed him to the floor. Arky sprang back to his feet, lowered his head and charged. He couldn't let Bear and the computer be captured. His head connected with the man's hip and it hurt. Arky was briefly stunned but he'd managed to thrust the man sideways and off balance, so Bear struggled free.

The man turned and leapt at Bear and the computer. Bear screamed loudly and Arky pulled him towards the door. But the man cut them off. With eyes flashing menace, he advanced.

Arky stepped back. 'Get away!' he yelled. 'Security is keeping watch on our room. You'd better run!'

'Security has its price,' the man growled. Then, he leapt at Bear and brutally tackled him to the ground. The man hauled a winded Bear to his feet and pinned him firmly under one strong arm. He wrenched the computer from Bear's grip and made a rush for the door.

But Arky raced around and got between the man and the door. He didn't know what he was going to do but he had to stop the man somehow.

Suddenly the door opened. Mia stood there, clutching her baseball bat.

Mia screamed in fright. Arky hurled himself at her, snatching the bat. Furiously, he turned and faced down their assailant. Mia turned and ran down the corridor yelling for help.

Arky swung the bat at the man's head. The man dropped Bear and swung the computer up to protect his head. The bat smashed into the laptop, shattering it. The man bolted into the corridor and disappeared down the fire stairs.

Arky and Bear burst fom the elevator and ran towards Doc and the others at the rooftop restaurant. Mia came after them and ran to her mother. 'Someone attacked us!' Arky said, still feeling terrified.

Alice gave Bear a hug while Arky explained what had happened. He felt guilty about looking at Doc's computer but Doc didn't seem angry. He was more worried about the attack.

'In fact,' he said as Alice rang Lieutenant Gatto, 'if the room had been empty the thief would have known how to break into the safe and would have taken the computer anyway. At least you stopped the artefact thieves getting the jump on us.'

When Lieutenant Gatto and Corporal Topi arrived, Arky and Bear told their story once again while Alice made some more phone calls. Lieutenant Gatto nodded seriously and looked at Doc. 'The boys say the man was after your computer, and you say you had a map and notes on that computer that showed where a lost city might be found, but who would know about it?'

Doc shrugged helplessly. 'I have no idea.'

'Maybe someone at the museum?' Arky said.

'Or someone who gave you your permission to go into the jungle,' Corporal Topi said. 'But now the computer is broken, I don't think they'll be a problem any more. You should be safe now.'

'Only the people in this room and Bear's stepfather, Lord Wright, knew about the information that was on the computer,' Doc said. 'Lord Wright was funding the trek. He got the permissions for us and he kept everything very quiet.'

'Maybe there was a spy,' Arky said, looking around.

'I don't think these bandits were after the computer.' Lieutenant Gatto spoke over Arky, dismissing his suggestion. 'I think young Bear here is worth more than the computer, even with its tantalising information. After all, it is highly unlikely that there really is a lost city.

'The boys say the man grabbed Bear and Bear was holding the computer. I would guess that Suarez has found out that you are staying here. Someone has talked about Bear. Bribery is big business, sadly. Bear's mother is very famous, and everyone knows she is married to Lord Wright and he is a very wealthy man. I think Bear was the target, not your computer. Suarez is famous for kidnapping people and getting ransoms.'

'I think,' said Alice, who had finally got off the phone, 'it is now too dangerous for us to stay. I have booked an earlier flight that leaves tonight.' She looked pointedly at Doc. 'And, I've also booked a seat for you, Lukas.'

Doc nodded, his mouth set in a grim line. 'I agree with my wife. Going on with our expedition would be stupid now. We will leave immediately.' He turned to Pancho. 'I'm sorry, Pancho, but perhaps when all the fuss has died down we could try again. We've had too much attention drawn to us now, so going anywhere would be foolish. I'll make sure you and the men you organised are paid for any trouble or time lost.'

Pancho was obviously disappointed and nodded weakly. 'I am sorry you are going, Doctor Steele,' he said. 'But if you must go, then at least allow me to drive you to the airport.'

Mia, who had been silent, burst into tears. 'And what about me and my mother?' she asked.

'Mia! Don't be so rude.' Camilla looked embarrassed.

'I will make sure you will be safe while you are in town.' Gatto patted Mia's hair.

'I'll have Pancho drive you and Camilla home tomorrow,' Doc said. He turned to Camilla. 'You have been through a lot lately because of us, so I'll make sure you have some extra money to help your family and I will keep in touch and find you another job.'

Camilla's face lit up. 'You have been very kind to us, Doctor Steele.'

Mia dried her tears. 'Thank you,' she said, reaching her hand out to the boys. 'I will say goodbye then, but I wish you had found time to play baseball.'

'Perhaps Mia could come with us to the airport?' Arky felt sad they were saying goodbye.

'Mia has never seen planes take off.' Camilla smiled. 'I think she would love to go.'

'Pancho, you wouldn't mind an extra passenger, would you?' asked Doc.

'She has helped save my life, how could I not do anything but treat her as my princess?' Pancho bowed to Mia, but Arky noticed his smile didn't seem to match his words.

Two Bandit Gangs

Goran Rulec was admiring one of his most treasured artefacts, Genghis Khan's golden Hand of Death, stolen from the Mongolian Government on Doctor Steele's last expedition.

Rulec was turning the treasure over when his private line rang. He placed the hand in a crystal case and picked up the phone. His eyes darkened with anger as his man in Central America began talking.

'What do you mean the computer is smashed? Unbelievable! So, now you tell me Doctor Steele is leaving tonight. You bungler!' He sucked his breath in, thinking how to solve the problem. 'This Suarez has ruined everything. There is only one thing you can do now: make Steele show you where the city lies. He knows where it is and how to find it, computer or not! Kidnap him. Take his family too and use them as leverage. He'll do as he's told, if they are at risk.'

Rulec wiped a stray lock of his wispy hair away from his eyes, listening as the caller complained about the order. 'No arguments! Don't let the brats worry you. You can snatch them on the way to the airport. Your own survival depends on it. Make sure they all disappear once we have what we want!' Rulec slammed the phone down and glared angrily into space.

Later, Corporal Topi rang Suarez. 'Yes, I tell you, they are leaving tonight. Their man Pancho is driving them. And now I know what Doctor Steele was looking for: a lost city!' Topi smiled at Suarez's reaction. 'Only Steele knows where to look. We have to get him before he leaves for the airport. He can lead you there. Think of the riches if we find it! And you can get your revenge.' Topi imagined how much money a lost city would bring—he could retire and live in luxury. 'Get cars and men ready. I'll let you know when they leave the hotel. Once they are kidnapped we can organise what we need to travel into the jungle.'

❖

As the traffic roared around the limousine on the way to the airport, Alice handed out icy poles. Mia stared at the treat in surprise and copied the way Arky and Bear unwrapped the paper covering. She put her lips on the cold sweet and her face lit up with such joy that Bear started laughing. Arky laughed even more as the top of Bear's icy pole melted and a big dollop landed on his shirt.

As Arky was watching Mia enjoy herself, an old blue car pulled sharply into the lane beside them, causing the limousine to swerve. Pancho honked his horn, but the the car just pulled closer.

'Slow down,' Doc said. 'Let him pass. We don't need any road rage.'

'I can't slow down,' Pancho said, looking in the rear-view mirror. 'There's a big truck behind us, and it is right on my bumper bar.'

Arky looked at the car beside them. There were four men inside. He paled. 'There's a man with a gun!' he cried.

'Speed up, Pancho.' Alice sounded worried. 'Maybe we can outrun them.'

'I can't,' Pancho said. 'We are hemmed in. The car in front of us is slowing down.' As he spoke, the three vehicles around them coordinated their speed and forced the limousine to the side of the road. They came to a halt. The passenger door of the old blue car opened and a young man with a closely shaven head leapt out. He pointed his gun at Pancho. 'Open the door and get out!'

'Do as he says,' Doc said. 'I don't want anyone killed.'

Pancho got out and was instantly hauled into the blue car, where three other men waited. The young man pointed the gun at Doc. 'You're driving,' he ordered. Doc undid his seatbelt and moved across to the driver's seat. The man turned his gun on Alice. 'You take the passenger seat.'

Alice moved from the back seat to sit beside Doc in the front and the young man moved around to the other side of the car and sat beside Mia and Bear. Arky was squashed up against the opposite window. The man kept his gun pointed at Alice in front. Mia began crying in fear.

Arky's icy pole melted down his hand and their kidnapper put his head out the window and called out in Spanish to the waiting henchmen. Then he spoke to Doc. 'Now we are ready to go. You do as I say or your wife will suffer.' Arky noticed the young man had a skull tattooed on the back of his neck.

'Go where?' Doc asked. He was visibly pale and his hands were shaking.

'Doctor Steele, you had a trip planned. We want you to keep to your plan. I think you know exactly where to go. The truck behind us is full of equipment for a lovely tour of the jungle. We are eight men and we all have guns. I would not try to trick us or escape.'

Doc nodded hopelessly and started the car. As they drove out into the jungle, Arky noticed Skull-head was leaning forward and keeping his eyes firmly on Doc and Alice. Arky's mother's handbag was still on the seat inbetween Mia and Bear, who were squashed against the young man. Inside the bag was his mother's new mobile. He couldn't reach it, but Bear could.

He reached over and gently prodded Bear. Bear turned to look at him, his eyes big with fear. Arky carefully mimed making a call on a phone, hoping the man beside them wouldn't see the gesture.

Bear caught the idea and nodded. Arky cautiously pointed at Alice's bag. Bear slid the zip open, centimetre by slow centimetre. He slipped his hand inside and pulled out the phone. He then slid the phone to Arky, who already had removed Lieutenant Gatto's card from his pocket.

Arky placed the phone down low and sent a text to Gatto's number: 'help kidnppd 2 cars 1 trk 8 men lookn for lost city in jungle.' He pushed send. The message went. Then, just as he breathed a sigh of relief, the phone began to ring. Arky jumped out of his skin as the ringtone reverberated through the car. Panicked, Mia screamed so shrilly that Arky's ears hurt.

Skull-head turned fast and, with terrifying fury, grabbed the phone, opened the window and hurled it out. 'Any other phones?' he shouted, over Mia's sobs. Doc frantically reached into his pocket and handed over his mobile. It also went out the window. Skull-head put his hand on Mia's shoulder. 'If you make one more sound, you'll follow the phones,' he said. Arky believed him.

Mia took a deep breath and stopped screaming, but tears poured down her face. Bear put his arm around her protectively.

'If you harm one hair on their heads,' Alice said angrily from the front seat, 'we won't help you. Then you'll have to shoot us, and you'll have nothing!'

Her voice was so strong and brave that Arky knew she wasn't bluffing. The man with the tattoo also knew. 'Good children won't be harmed.' He smiled at the children, showing his teeth. 'You don't want your parents hurt and they don't want you hurt. If you all play that game, then all will be well.'

What Skull-head didn't know was that three more cars full of bandits were following them. In one of these cars was Suarez, who was suffering from another attack of rage after witnessing the kidnapping.

'Who has them?' he shouted into his phone. 'We were about to stop them, when a truck and two other cars came from nowhere and took them. Now they are driving out into the jungle. What is happening? Who else is bribing you?'

'No one knows other than you.' Corporal Topi was surprised. 'I have told no one. My boss has just rung me to say he got a message from Mrs Steele's phone to say they have been kidnapped. He says there are eight men and a truck, and they are going to look for the lost city. They have the doctor, his wife and the children as hostages.'

'I know that!' Suarez shouted. 'I'm behind the truck myself with twelve men.'

'Then you have the advantage. Get rid of the other kidnappers,' Corporal Topi said. 'Then you will have all the equipment to go into the jungle and find the lost city for yourself.'

Suarez hung up on him.

Betrayed

Doc drove for hours, guided by the GPS Skull-head provided. They travelled through small towns where dogs leapt out and barked at the passing convoy. Eventually, they were driving in the dark. Fields and farmhouse lights vanished behind them.

Finally they came to a dirt track that led deep into the mountains. Their headlights cut the inky jungle darkness, occasionally highlighting wild animals that darted out of the way.

As tree branches swished against the car and Arky was jolted in his seat, he couldn't help but wonder what was going to happen to them when they stopped. The lost city was hidden somewhere in the rough, mountainous jungle ahead and Arky was pretty sure Skull-head wouldn't want them coming with him. What would he do? A shiver of fear made the hairs on Arky's body rise. He looked over at Bear, who was biting his lips. He hoped his mum and dad were planning something to help them escape.

Sometime after midnight, the track ran out and Doc stopped the car. 'This is where we were going to start our trek,' he announced. 'But there is no point going anywhere without plenty of supplies.'

'We'll sleep here tonight.' Skull-head ignored Doc's words. He ordered everyone out of their car as the other vehicles pulled up behind them. Arky and Bear bundled out. Arky had been sitting so long his legs shook and he was busting for a pee.

Skull-head obviously had the same problem because he headed for the trees. Without a word, Alice and Mia dashed in the opposite direction and disappeared behind some bushes. Arky, Bear and Doc hurriedly followed Skull-head.

When they returned, Skull-head's men had opened the truck and were pulling out tents and camping equipment. Car headlights and torches lit their activity. Arky noticed Pancho sitting in the old blue car, but he didn't get out. 'Is he alive?' he asked Doc.

'He's probably been told not to move,' Doc replied. 'We are the valuable ones so they will look after us. Pancho might be tied up.'

Once the camp was set up, a gas stove was lit and the scent of coffee filled the air. The prisoners were offered food and drink and shown to a tent. 'You'll all sleep here,' Skull-head said. 'Don't think of escaping. You are well guarded.'

Knowing it was useless to try to talk reason to their kidnappers, Doc and Alice followed the man's orders. Once inside the cramped tent, Mia, Bear and Arky squeezed in between Alice and Doc.

'How far to the lost city?' Arky whispered.

'I don't actually know if it exists and I don't know where it is,' Doc replied. 'As you know, the diary was written by a man who had a terrible fever and was lost. I'm making an educated guess as to the general area.'

'Will they leave us behind?' Bear asked.

'I think we should try to stay together,' Alice replied. 'It wouldn't be good to separate.'

Bear wriggled, trying to get comfy. 'If you don't find the city, what then?'

Arky felt his mother stiffen against him at the question.

'Try to sleep,' said Doc, giving Bear a hug. 'We'll have to keep our wits about us tomorrow. Fresh brains are the best.' There was no argument from the boys, but Mia began a little prayer in Spanish.

Arky shut his eyes and was willing sleep to come, when a sudden volley of shots made everyone jump. Torchlights cut through the dark, lighting the tent fabric. '*Policia!*' yelled a voice. '*Que están rodeado.*'

'The police,' Mia translated. 'They have surrounded us!'

'Keep down,' Doc hissed, pushing his arm across Arky and Bear and holding them to the ground as more shots rang out. The surprised bandits began shouting and running for their lives.

Arky was thrilled. His message to Lieutenant Gatto had worked. Somehow he had tracked them down. Soon they would be freed.

Seconds later there were more shots and Arky heard Skull-head cry out in pain. '*Nos damos por vencidos!*'

'They are giving up!' Mia said. 'We are saved!'

'Stay still,' warned Alice. 'Wait till the police open up the tent and tell us it is safe. One of the bandits might try to hurt us in revenge if we move too soon.'

Everyone lay still while the bandits were captured, in a hubbub of noise and shouting. Finally, someone came to the tent and opened the flap. A torch shone into Arky's eyes, blinding him.

'Here they are,' called a voice. 'Five little pigeons, waiting for us.'

'Suarez!' Doc cried out.

Suarez ordered everyone out of the tent. Arky took in the torch-lit scene. He instantly recognised the huge four-fingered man who had attacked them at the hotel. He was now standing over Skull-head with a gun. Skull-head was bound and bleeding from a wound on his arm. His men were also trussed up, along with Pancho.

Suarez marched along the row of imprisoned men, inspecting their faces. He stopped in front of Pancho, recognising him immediately. 'What are you doing here? Aren't you an archaeologist?'

'I was kidnapped by these men.' Pancho sounded angry. 'They kept me prisoner in their car. I'm not one of them.'

Suarez turned to Doc. 'Is this true?'

'Yes,' replied Doc. 'Pancho was removed from our car when they kidnapped us.'

'Untie him,' Suarez ordered. Pancho's bonds were cut and he clambered shakily to his feet, glaring at the men who had captured him.

Suarez then ordered his men to unpack the truck. When it was empty, they manhandled the kidnappers into the back. As Skull-head was being hauled into the truck, Pancho suddenly broke free, yelling like a crazy man. Pancho lunged at Skull-head, grabbing him by the shirt and shaking him furiously. 'This will serve you right!' he roared. 'You will know how horrible it is to be held prisoner!'

Suarez's bandits pulled Pancho away, laughing at his anger, and dragged him back to Doc and Alice.

Arky was shocked by Pancho's sudden rage. It seemed out of character with the cheerful person he had come to know. Pancho was puffing loudly and his face was dark with anger. Alice patted his shoulder, while Doc put a comforting arm around him.

Arky looked back to the truck. Skull-head seemed to have found the incident amusing and was smiling as Suarez's bandits hauled him into the truck.

Suarez locked the metal truck doors and threw away the key. 'It will be very hot in there and there is no water.' He laughed. 'They'll cook to death. That will save us some bullets.'

'I can't believe we've been kidnapped three times in as many days,' Doc said, still soothing Pancho. 'These men are very cruel, but we have children with us. We can't afford to get angry with anyone. We have to have our wits about us if we are to escape with our lives.'

Suarez overheard Doc and approached. He stood in front of Bear, and lifted his chin. His eyes were black and beady. Bear looked worried. 'I don't think you'll escape, but you might get away with your lives if your rich relative pays,' he said. 'And, Doctor Steele, you must make me happy by finding this lost city. But if you try to escape, then Pancho might not live so long. And this little girl is worthless . . . so, you can see my position.'

Mia let out a sob and Alice pressed the girl to her. 'Don't cry, Mia,' she said calmly. 'We'll not let anyone hurt you. Don't think about bad things. You have already proven how brave you are—and brave people win.'

Pancho glared at Suarez as he was thrown a blanket and led off to share a tent with his new captors.

Suarez turned to Doc. 'Get back to sleep,' he ordered. 'You have a lot to do tomorrow.'

Arky tried to sleep, but he was too wound up by the day's events. There were also several puzzles playing on his mind. One puzzle was that Skull-head had told Arky in the car that he was part of a gang of eight. Yet, only seven men had been locked in the truck. Where was the missing man?

Also, how had Suarez found them? Perhaps one of the kidnappers was a traitor, working for Suarez. It could explain how Suarez had sneaked up on them and why there were only seven men in the truck—because the eighth man was now part of Suarez's gang. But how did two gangs know about their movements? Even more puzzling to Arky was that both gangs knew about the lost city. Someone is a spy, thought Arky, and he was sure that person was Lieutenant Gatto.

Lieutenant Gatto was shocked when he received the text from Alice Steele's phone saying they had been kidnapped. He couldn't believe it could happen again, so quickly. Someone had to have tipped the bandits off about Doctor Steele's movements. Gatto sent out people to search for them and quickly discovered they had not reached the airport and the phone message was real. By the time he had organised a manhunt, it was too late—they had vanished.

Gatto assumed Suarez had struck again, but this time he obviously knew about Doctor Steele's plans and the lost city. Not for the first time, Gatto suspected that someone in the police force was giving Suarez information. He made a decision not to give anyone—not even his trusted sidekick, Coporal Topi—any more information.

He started to form a plan, believing that Suarez's greed could be his undoing. Gatto suspected Suarez had previously sold his ill-gotten gains to illegal dealers or middlemen who shipped the stolen goods out of the country. Gatto had always been too busy to hunt down these middlemen, but this time he'd try to find the exporter and, through him, Suarez.

The first thing Gatto did was contact Lord Wright, Bear's stepfather, to tell him the terrible news. Lord Wright was surprisingly practical and businesslike, not at all like a panicked parent. He asked Gatto to keep the story away from the news and said he would fly out to help with the investigation immediately. Gatto organised to have him picked up at the airport the following day.

When Lieutenant Gatto told Mia's mother, Camilla, about the kidnapping, the poor woman wept with terror. She cheered up a little when he told her that Lord Wright was going to help him get Mia and the others back.

Finally, Lieutenant Gatto went to the museum to tell them that Suarez had abducted their employee, Pancho Alverez. He came away from his meeting with the museum supervisor very worried indeed.

Lord Wright and Bear's mother, Linda Redford, the famous actress, arrived in the city the next day. Lord Wright hired a hotel room and had a meeting with Lieutenant Gatto almost immediately. After deep discussion and planning, he agreed with Gatto that they should act alone and try to rescue the hostages. He also agreed not to involve anyone else in the police force.

'If Doctor Steele finds the lost city,' Lieutenant Gatto said, 'Suarez doesn't have the resources to sell all the artefacts himself.'

Lord Wright nodded in agreement. 'He will have a whole city to plunder. That will mean a lot of goods to move. Suarez will have to take them to dealers to ship them.'

'The artefacts would have to be smuggled out of the country,' Gatto said, 'and they will have to be stored somewhere. I think we should look for a warehouse near a port.' He looked grimly at Lord Wright. 'Once Suarez has begun to sell his stolen goods he will then try to ransom off his hostages. We are taking a risk that he won't kill them as soon as they find the city.'

Lord Wright bit his bottom lip. 'Doctor Steele is very resourceful and so is his wife,' he said, obviously distressed. 'The boys are also very sensible. They've come through some dangerous experiences in the past, so I have faith they will stay alive.' He picked up his phone. 'I have a lot of contacts and I will hire detectives to look for appropriate buildings. Once we identify the buildings, I will make sure they are watched around the clock. I will also hire a group of ex-military security guards to act if we see anything suspicious.' He shook Gatto's hand. 'These men will all be hand-picked and can be trusted. With your help, I think we will find my stepson and my friends.'

The private phone on Goran Rulec's desk rang, startling him. Rulec worked on the idea that no news was good news. If it was his man in Central America, then it meant the kidnapping of Doctor Steele had failed. If that were the case, there would be one less man in Central America tomorrow morning. He'd get someone else to run his warehouse filled with prized antiques and treasures that were ready to be shipped to special clients.

He picked up the phone, his eyebrows furrowed.

'Lord Wright has suddenly cancelled all business meetings and his wife Linda has suspended all her engagements,' said a voice. It was the spy that Rulec had planted in Lord Wright's house. 'They've both flown to Central America. It looks like Belvedere has been kidnapped, along with Doctor Steele and his family.'

'How terrible.' Rulec smiled. 'Perhaps you could let me know if there is anything I can do to help the poor man at this difficult time.' He put the phone down.

Success! He rubbed his hands together.

Rulec could barely wait to find out if there really was a lost city. If there was, he would have the pick of all the best treasures. Either way, city or not, Bear and the Steeles would vanish and he'd finally really hurt Lord Wright.

Terrible Gods

Arky awoke as Doc and Alice clambered out of the tent. It took him a moment to realise the sounds outside came from Suarez and his men preparing for their jungle trek. Bear rubbed his eyes and Mia sat up. 'We better get outside too,' Arky said.

Pancho was already opening bags and sorting food supplies under Suarez's supervision when Arky stepped out of the tent. Muffled bangs and groans came from inside the truck where Skull-head and his men lay trapped. Arky worried about what might happen next, but there was nothing he could do except help his parents check the supplies that were scattered beside the cars and around the tents.

Eventually, backpacks full of food, tents, cooking equipment, ropes and knives lay on the ground, ready to go.

Doc, Alice and Pancho huddled close to the boys and waited for Suarez's commands.

'That truck was full of everything Pancho and I ordered for our expedition,' Doc whispered. 'That must mean that someone at the museum controls the first lot of kidnappers.'

'Could Rulec be behind it?' Arky eyed off two child-size backpacks in the pile of provisions. 'Lord Wright was funding your expedition to find the lost city and we know Rulec watches his every move. The first lot of kidnappers somehow knew we were going to the airport, and they knew Bear and I were with you. Otherwise, why would there be kids' packs over there? You rang Lord Wright and told him we were flying out! So, they had to organise the kidnapping after that.'

'Arky's right. Someone has very good knowledge of our movements,' Alice said.

'And Suarez?' Bear interjected. 'How does he fit in?'

'I think he's an opportunistic thug,' Pancho replied.

'And he wants me for ransom.' Bear looked really upset. 'It's my fault we are all here. I'm so sorry.'

'It's not your fault.' Alice put her hand on Bear's shoulder. 'We are all in this together, one way or the other.'

Pancho said, 'You're the added value, Bear, but someone in the police must have tipped Saurez off about the lost city. That's why there are two gangs fighting over us.'

'It must have been Inspector Gatto,' Arky moaned. 'I texted him and told him we were being kidnapped. Then the next thing we knew, Suarez found us!'

Doc and Alice gave Arky a sympathetic hug.

'You did the right thing,' Doc said. 'You weren't to know. In fact, Suarez might be better to deal with than Rulec's men. Suarez will look after us in the jungle. We're worth money to him. If the traitor in the museum had us, I suspect we may never have left the jungle once the city was found.'

'But we can't be sure,' Alice said. 'We will have to try to escape. It would be too dangerous to just let them control us.'

'We will try,' Doc said. 'If we can't find the lost city, we must make them think it's there or they could turn nasty. We have to keep them busy while we think of ways to get rid of them. I'll try to unsettle them.' A mischievous glint lit his eyes. 'Lost cities are full of ghosts and these men are very superstitious.'

Doc led the way towards the ravine through a chaotic mass of impenetrable plants, using the GPS. Suarez's henchmen used machetes to hack into the vines and tendrils, cutting a path. The ravine was steep. The men, carrying large packs, were slowed down as they slipped and slid down the escarpment. Within minutes the jungle became a steam bath. Amongst the trees, hummingbirds and bright parrots called and fluttered. Giant spiders hung in massive cobwebs and, although the odd one dropped on them, Arky discovered they didn't bite.

Bear was stuck behind Mia, who fell several times and grazed her knees. It wasn't long before Arky noticed Bear was helping her over the biggest fallen logs. He couldn't help smiling.

Alice was probably the worst off, because she had only had time to buy a few clothes before they had been kidnapped again. Her shoes were flat-heeled, but her light, short-sleeved blouse allowed every insect within miles to sample her blood. Within an hour her arms were covered in red blotches, despite the repellent that Doc had put on everyone before breakfast.

Doc soon noticed her distress and gave her his shirt. He bent down and slathered oozing mud over his chest and arms. He said it helped keep the biting creatures away.

By midmorning Suarez called a halt beside a massive fallen tree that had ripped other trees from the ground and created a small clearing. It also gave them their first view of the landscape below. Doc turned and smiled reassuringly at Mia, Arky and Bear, pointing the way ahead. 'See, below us is a snake-like river and to one side of it we can see a swamp.' He lifted his hand and pointed to a smoking volcano with twin vents. 'I believe we can bypass the swamp, cross the river further up and head towards the volcano.'

'That would be another four days hacking through the jungle before we begin our hunt,' Suarez said, mentally counting the packs and supplies.

'Yes,' Alice said, reading his thoughts. 'You have too many men and not enough food. The truck was packed for us and eight bandits, not thirteen.'

'Then you will be on half rations,' Suarez snarled.

Long after Suarez and his captives left the truck and cars behind, Skull-head and his men struggled to free themselves from their bonds. The terrible heat inside the truck took its toll and a man fainted. It took hours for the first of the kidnappers to wriggle free. He was quick to release Skull-head and then the others. Once Skull-head rubbed his numb hands back to life, he stood shakily and felt in his shirt pocket. He smiled as he took a key from inside and unlocked a small inspection hatch leading from the cargo hold to the driver's cabin. The men squeezed through the portal, dragged themselves into the cabin and climbed outside.

'Now what do we do?' asked one of the men. 'Take the cars and get out of here?'

Skull-head thrust his jaw out angrily. 'We take the cars and go to the nearest town. Then we get more supplies and guns. Their trail should be easy to follow. We will ambush them once they find the city!'

As night fell, Suarez ordered his men to hack out a small clearing in the jungle and the tents were erected. A smoky fire was lit to keep the hungry insects away. Arky thought the sounds of the jungle were as loud as city traffic—with the humming and pinging of insects, the cries of night birds rustling in the trees overhead and the terrified shriek of a monkey surprised by a hunting animal. All of these sounds pressed in on him. And the insects swarming around and eating each other added to Arky's sense of discomfort.

There was a weird cough nearby and Suarez's men leapt to their feet, aiming their guns into the inky blackness.

'They're afraid a jaguar will eat one of them for dinner,' Pancho said. 'They are afraid of jaguars.'

'How interesting . . .' A faint smile crossed Doc's face. He winked at the children. Arky wondered what he was planning.

A hair-raising, ghostly cry came from the jungle. Arky thought it could have been an owl, but it made the bandits very restless.

Doc, sensing their fear, leant over to Suarez. 'After we cross the river tomorrow,' he said, 'we will go through the jungle to the edge of the volcano. I'd like your men to look out for carvings of jaguars.'

'Jaguars?' Suarez sounded puzzled.

'Carved in stone,' Doc said. 'It will be the first sign we are getting close to finding the clues to the hidden city left by Pezaro, the conquistador. He says the body of his friend, Francisco, is in the care of a jaguar and he hid a special box close by.'

'Why do we need this box?' Suarez asked.

'It contains a drawing that will help us find the lost city amongst all the deep chasms and valleys near the volcano. We could waste years trying to find the city without it.'

'Why jaguars?' Arky asked, knowing Doc would have a good story. 'Why did people carve jaguars?'

'There was a Toltec god called Tezcatlipoca,' Doc said, making sure his voice carried to the bandits.

'Tezcatal-whatsipa?' asked Bear. 'That's like talking in barbed wire. What's it mean?'

'Smoking mirror,' answered Doc. 'He was a god who took several animal shapes but was mostly drawn as a jaguar. He carried a smoking obsidian mirror. Human skulls, covered in jade, were dedicated to him. I believe he is the god they worshipped in the city we are looking for.'

'What sort of god was he?' Bear was clearly hoping for one of Doc's history stories.

Arky noticed Suarez's bandits had stopped talking and were listening.

'A terrible god!' Doc made his voice sound frightening—even Arky flinched. 'Tezcatlipoca was the starter of wars. He loves darkness and brings death and destruction. Even mentioning his name brings him close.' As if on cue, a jaguar in the jungle coughed. Its throaty presence made the hairs on Arky's neck rise. The bandits shifted nervously.

'Human sacrifices were practised in his name,' Doc continued. 'It is said that he creeps from the shadows and kills bad folk with a terrible disease known as the ghost sickness.'

'Ghost sickness?' Mia's voice was filled with terror.

Arky leant over and put his arm around her. 'Don't let the story frighten you,' he whispered. 'Doc's smart—he'll make the story spooky and try to unsettle the bandits.'

Out in the jungle beyond them an animal, perhaps a wild pig, screamed in agony. The jaguar had found its prey.

'The jaguar god stalks all evil men,' Doc said, his voice rising 'and—'

'Enough!' Suarez shouted. 'We do not need to hear silly stories.'

Before Arky finally fell asleep, he worried how Doc and Pancho would find one ancient rotted body in one of the wildest jungles in the world. It was an almost impossible task, worse than a needle in a haystack. But Arky knew his father must have some clue in his mind as to where Francisco's body might be. Doc was renowned for his knowledge of old legends, so Arky was sure he knew much more than he was letting on.

Arky fell asleep wondering what the Spanish conquistador, Alfonso Pezaro, meant when he had written: 'I placed Francisco's body in care of a jaguar and let a monster swallow the jade box. I left the sorcerer's dagger to open the way.'

The following day, Arky and Bear followed Doc and the others over dense creepers where the earth became sticky with decaying leaves. The sound of the rushing water of the river grew closer and the trees and creepers vanished, replaced by swamp. The sun lit their way but the swampy earth stuck to their feet and clung to their legs, making every step difficult. Arky's legs were soon covered in mud but the adults, carrying heavy packs, sank further.

He and Bear helped haul Doc and Pancho towards the river, while Mia helped Alice.

To make things worse, snakes of every size slithered away as they struggled through the sticky swamp. At one stage, Arky and Bear were stopped in their tracks by a mighty beast of a snake, longer than a man. It lifted its tiny head and glared at them, then turned and slipped into the reeds. 'That's an anaconda,' Mia said. 'They strangle animals with their big muscles. Some grow longer than a car.'

Finally they emerged beside a fast-flowing river. Arky was so happy to soak his aching legs in the cool water. Suarez sent the bandit with a scarred face to scout along the shore. Scarface returned an hour later to say he'd found a shallow crossing, so everyone shouldered their packs again and followed him.

The crossing wasn't very wide, but the water was flowing fast. 'Keep an eye out for crocodiles,' Suarez ordered, pulling his gun out. 'Jose, Domingo,' he pointed to two of the bandits—a small man with a bushy beard and the four-fingered man who had tried to kidnap Bear. 'You hold on to the brats so no one is swept away.'

Bear found himself held tightly, once again, by Domingo, the four-fingered man with strong arms, while Mia was lifted onto the shoulders of Jose, the man with the bushy beard, and Arky was dragged between both men. The crossing was uneventful and they landed in a natural clearing in the jungle.

'We make camp here,' Suarez said, realising everyone was exhausted from their trek through the swamp.

That night, fires were lit and the bandits split up into small groups. Suarez posted a guard—Bear nicknamed him 'Squinty' because of his odd eyes— to sit by the shore to watch out for crocodiles.

As Arky was eating his meagre dinner, a slight movement in the shadows above one of the fires attracted his attention. Two bandits were underneath the shadow. He poked Bear. 'A big anaconda is above them,' he whispered.

Doc and Pancho overheard him and came closer. 'We can make this work for us,' Pancho said. 'We could frighten these men more.'

Doc nodded in agreement and turned to Arky. 'Ask me more about the smoking-mirror god.'

'Dad,' Arky said loudly, 'what else did the jaguar god do? Did he murder lots of people?'

'He was very nasty,' Doc replied. Arky noticed the men nearby shifted position to listen to the clever history doctor tell another story, and the anaconda crept ever closer. *They'll get a fright when they see that huge snake*, thought Arky.

'Sometimes, Smoking Mirror would change his shape and become Mixcoatl, or Cloud Serpent.'

'What was Cloud Serpent?' Bear asked, sounding a bit too excited. Pancho poked him hard.

'Cloud Serpent took the shape of a snake and was the god of sorcerers,' Doc said as the anaconda slithered out on a branch above the bandits. 'Cloud Serpent killed four hundred of his own children, and was the god of ambush. He would sneak up on his victims, who were huddling by their fires, cut their hearts out and, later, wear his victims' skin as a cloak.'

At Doc's words, the anaconda slithered directly over one of the men. Arky was about to shout a warning to the bandits, when Pancho clamped his hand over his mouth.

Doc was shocked at Pancho's action and grabbed Pancho's hand. He didn't see the snake as it dropped onto the bandit and wrapped itself around the man's neck.

'Snake!' Bear yelled, astonished that the snake had actually attacked a man beside a fire just like in the story, but his cry was too late. The bandit fell silently to the ground as the snake wound itself around his neck. Wrapped in giant squirming scales, the man writhed on the ground in a death struggle.

Suarez's bandits grabbed their guns and raced to help. Shots rang out and the snake's head exploded, but its terrible coils continued to twist with horrific strength around its prey. Several men fell upon the snake, hauling it from the man. But it was too late.

Suarez turned angrily on Doc. 'You tell one more story,' he yelled, 'and it will be your last!'

The Jaguar

The following morning the bandits left their campfires and their breakfasts bubbling in pots and went to bury their amigo. Arky, seeing the men digging the grave, wandered unhappily around the camp. Bear and Mia noticed his mood and joined him. After several moments of walking in silence, Arky finally said, 'The jungle is a really scary place.'

'The bandits are scarier,' Bear said. But then he realised his friend was upset about the man who had been killed by the anaconda. He put his arm around Arky's shoulder and added, 'You shouldn't feel bad. That snake was hunting. He would have got that bad guy anyway.'

'But we could have warned him.' Arky heaved a sigh. 'Pancho shouldn't have stopped me. It's terrible to think one of them died and we saw it coming.'

'I might die,' Mia said quietly. 'The bandits don't need me. That man would have killed me quicker than that snake killed him if Suarez ordered him to. Pancho is just trying to save us.'

'I agree,' Bear said. 'We have one less nasty person around. He would have hurt us and we have to try . . .' His voice trailed away as an enormous, yellow-spotted slug dropped off a branch above his head and fell onto his shoulder. 'Yuck!' Bear flicked the creature at Mia. It landed on her forehead and slipped down her nose, making Arky laugh. Shuddering, Mia picked it up and threw it at Arky.

The slug landed on Arky's neck. He threw the slimy blob back at Bear, who ducked.

A pot of soup, bubbling on a nearby fire waiting for the bandits' return, welcomed the odd creature with a 'plop'. The slug disappeared in a small cloud of bubbles.

'Oops,' said Bear, staring at the soup.

'We should get it out,' Arky said. 'It might make someone sick.'

'Good!' Bear smiled. 'I hope it does.'

Arky made a step towards the soup, but Bear looked over his shoulder and saw the bandits returning to the camp. 'Don't Arky,' he warned. 'If they see us fiddling with their soup they'll think we did it on purpose. Let's go! They'll see the slug and toss it out.'

The boys returned to their campfire and waited for Squinty and Scarface, whose breakfast was in the pot, to see the slug and throw it away. But the men poured their soup into cups and drank it down without a grimace.

'The slug must have disintegrated,' Arky said.

'Must have tasted all right,' Bear added, rather surprised.

After breakfast, Arky and Bear shouldered their packs and followed the others up the hill towards the volcano and the looming cliffs. It was difficult going and they had not travelled far when several bandits began waving their hands in front of their noses.

'*Dejar de pedos!*' they cried, shouting at Squinty.

'Get to the back,' Suarez yelled, pointing to the men who had drunk the slug soup. 'We don't need stinky men poisoning the air in front of us.'

The men obeyed, emitting loud gaseous noises as they went. As the group kept labouring through the jungle, the farting men began to attract blowflies. The buzzing insects clouded around them. At first the other bandits laughed mightily but, as the flies settled on Squinty's and Scarface's backs and attacked their eyes, the laughter faded.

Pancho, seeing the two men surrounded by a fuzzy cloud, said very loudly. 'They look like walking ghosts! Perhaps this is the ghost sickness we heard about!'

The other bandits glanced at the men again, looking worried.

By late afternoon the expedition had reached the first cliffs under the volcano and the exploding, fly-ridden men had fallen a long way behind.

Suarez called a halt in a natural clearing filled with moss-covered boulders. Everyone gratefully sat down and rested, waiting for Squinty and Scarface to catch up. When they arrived everyone set to and erected their tents for the night.

When the camp was set up and wood for the fires had been gathered, Doc asked Alice, Arky, Bear and Mia if they'd like to look around the campsite. 'We'll look for any signs of an ancient civilisation,' he said. 'Examine rocky overhangs or big rocks carefully, or anything that can be used for graffiti. People all through the ages liked to leave marks on blank walls.'

Doc, who had lots of practice in finding ancient relics, was the first to notice something on one of the rocks, overgrown with moss. He excitedly rubbed the plants away. Alice cried out with surprise as a picture of a man, emerging like a ghost from the body of a jaguar, was revealed. Arky and Bear studied the carving and were quick to notice that the carved man wore a face mask and carried arrows and a knife.

'This is the sort of carving I was hoping to find.' Doc smiled. 'It proves I was right about the diary.'

'Is the city nearby?' Mia asked.

'I think so,' replied Doc. 'In the Spanish Diary, Pezaro says Francisco died where the jungle started. I'm confident about his diary being true now that we've found this carving. The city must be hidden above the tree line.'

'Do we tell the bandits?' Arky asked.

Doc nodded. 'Tomorrow we'll need to hunt for jaguar sculptures. They will be well hidden by the jungle and we will need everyone's sharp eyes to find them.'

'Are you sure there will be jaguar sculptures here?' Bear asked, looking around at the overgrown vines and thick bushes. 'Pezaro may have meant he left his friend's body to be eaten by jaguars.'

'The diary is full of cryptic clues,' Arky said thoughtfully. 'Pezaro wanted someone to look for a special jaguar that would *care* for a body. Dad's right—it must be a sculpture. And somewhere near Francisco's body there must be some sort of monster where the jade box is hidden.' He looked up at his father. 'It won't be easy, will it? The body of Francisco may have long rotted away.'

'Doc, could you find the city without the jade box and the drawing?' asked Bear.

'No.' Doc rubbed his chin anxiously with his hand. 'Pezaro says there are secret ways to enter the city. I will need the drawing.'

'Once you find it, though,' Alice said, looking very worried, 'we may be of no further use to Suarez.'

'The drawing will be useless to anyone who doesn't understand Toltec glyphs,' Doc said reassuringly. 'Also, I think there is a secret passageway into the city, which we will need the sorcerer's knife for, but I won't let them know that.'

'If Pancho can read the glyphs they still might not need us,' said Bear.

'I think they do need us,' Doc said. 'Pancho didn't read the diary so he doesn't know all the clues. And from what I've seen of Pancho, he has a lot to learn—he doesn't know the Toltec myths and legends and they will also be needed to understand the drawing. And I still believe Suarez will want us for ransom.'

'I am scared,' Mia said. 'They do not need me.'

'We'll protect you.' Bear smiled.

Doc rubbed Bear's hair and smiled, and then he turned around and called for Suarez.

'What is it?' Suarez moved towards them quickly. Several of his men and Pancho followed to see what had been discovered.

'It's the ghost of the Cloud Serpent,' Pancho said, pointing excitedly. 'It has been placed here to warn people away.'

'Yes,' agreed Doc. 'You can see his ghostly form shape-shifting from jaguar to serpent. There are many ghostly dangers ahead.'

The men instantly seemed to become tense, looking around the jungle nervously.

Suarez scowled at Doc. 'For the last time—shut up!'

The volcano above them rumbled ominously as night settled over the trees. The ground shook slightly and an eerie light from two lava vents near the top of the volcano made it appear like the mountain was watching them with demonic eyes. Squinty and Scarface, the two men still with flies hovering around them, pointed at shadows, crying out fearfully.

'They say the evil eyes are watching them and they will never sleep,' Pancho translated.

'It sounds more like they are delirious,' Doc said. 'I wonder how they got so sick?'

'A big slug dropped into their soup,' Bear said. 'I think it upset them.'

Pancho stroked his moustache and snorted with laughter. 'I must remember that.'

The following morning, while the two sick men remained in their tent, away from the flies, Doc held a meeting with Suarez. He explained that the time had come to find Francisco's body and the jade box with the ancient Toltec map or there was no way anyone could go further.

Suarez organised everyone into pairs and they set off to search for jaguars. Alice and Mia were together, Suarez kept Pancho by his side, and Domingo guarded Doc. Arky and Bear had pleaded to be allowed to go off on their own. 'We will leave marks on trees,' Arky said. 'We won't get lost!'

'We've got sharp eyes,' Bear added, 'and we won't go far away from the cliff. We can find the camp again easily!'

'You've managed well in the past . . .' Doc looked over at Alice, who smiled in agreement.

Suarez nodded and waved his machete. 'Make sure you return within an hour or your dad and Pancho might have an accident.'

The boys nodded.

Arky and Bear hurried off to hunt on their own. They wandered underneath the giant cliff until Arky noticed a shadow move in the undergrowth. He paused and pulled Bear's shirt. 'Look,' he whispered.

A spotted cub was leaping to catch a praying mantis. Seeing the boys, it stopped and turned. Its yellow eyes widened in fright and it hissed furiously.

'It's cute,' said Bear, admiring the animal, 'but where's its mum?'

A bigger shadow moved above them. Arky looked up. The largest creature, with the biggest teeth Arky had ever seen, snarled and leapt from a nearby tree to stand between the cub and Arky and Bear. The creature swiped the air with its claws and jumped forwards.

'Run!' Bear cried, turning and dashing into the jungle.

Arky raced after him and quickly overtook Bear. He glanced behind to check where the jaguar was, tripped and fell. He landed heavily, temporarily winded. Bear caught up to him.

It took Arky a few seconds to realise the animal hadn't chased them, but had taken its baby away to safety. He recovered from his fright and found his breath again, while Bear puffed nearby. From his low vantage point on the ground, Arky's eyes were attracted to a rather odd-looking mossy rock under a tree. It took him a few seconds to realise the rock had carved claws. He crawled forwards to investigate. 'Bear!' he shouted. 'Look!'

A jaguar carving, almost as big as the boys, was hidden under the roots of a giant tree.

'We should get back to camp and get Doc and Pancho,' Bear said.

'What if there are more though?' Arky said. 'Lets look over there, under the cliff first.' A shadowy overhang of rock jutted out from the steep cliffs, so Bear and Arky made their way towards it. They were rewarded. Under the overhang, protected from the rain, was a huge moss-covered stone jaguar with large carved wings.

'A flying jaguar!' cried Bear, excitedly.

The sculpture's eyes glared down at the boys as they climbed onto its large paws and peered at the creature's back. 'Look!' Arky pointed.

On the back of the jaguar, protected by its wings, were the remains of a man. His clothes had long rotted from his body. Only buttons and the odd buckle told the boys that the body had once worn European clothing. The skull's moss-filled eye sockets stared up at a large orchid growing in a crack in the rocks above. The skull's teeth were set in a horrible grin. 'It's got to be Francisco!' cried Arky, hauling himself up onto the jaguar's back beside the body. 'We've found him!'

On closer inspection, the boys noticed Francisco's feet had long gone, as had one leg, perhaps chewed off by some animal, but one hand was pinned by a pile of stones placed on the wrist. The skeletal fingers pointed to a tree further out in the jungle. 'We should look out there,' Arky said. 'It's a clue. He could be pointing to the monster!'

Arky and Bear tumbled down from the winged jaguar. Further into the ancient jungle, in the direction Francisco had been pointing, they discovered a huge statue with a jaguar's body and a fearsome serpent's head. The demonic creature had slitted eyes and an enormous mouth filled with hideous fangs, laced with spider webs.

'It fits with the Spanish Diary,' said Arky, in awe. 'Francisco's body is in the care of a jaguar. This must be the monster that swallowed the jade box. Its mouth is big enough.'

'I think we should get Doc,' Bear said, staring at the grim creature. 'I wouldn't like to go up there and amongst those big spiders without him around.'

The Jade Box

Arky and Bear had gathered Doc, Suarez and the other bandits. Alice and Mia had followed them into the jungle too and now everyone stood underneath the terrible snake-headed jaguar.

'You think there is a jade box with a map inside there?' Suarez was studying the sculpture carefully. 'I'll send a man up.' He motioned to Jose, with the bushy beard. 'You are the smallest.'

Jose reluctantly clambered up onto the jaguar god's back and slithered his way to its head. He brushed away the spiders, grabbed the fangs with his hands and slowly hauled himself into its mouth.

Arky thought it looked like Jose was being swallowed: only his feet were sticking out of the beast's mouth now.

A little while later, Jose's muffled, fearful voice floated down to the waiting group. 'I cannot fit. Someone smaller needs to go down.'

All eyes shifted to Arky. Doc leant over and whispered, 'You don't have to go unless you want to, but if you do, and you find the jade box, do not open it. Francisco opened it and died hours later. Handle it with care.'

Arky nodded. 'I'll be fine. If it's there, I'll get it.'

Domingo picked Arky up as if he were a feather and thrust him into the monster's mouth. Arky pulled himself inside using the giant fangs. The warm filtered light of the jungle was soon blotted out as he wriggled into the creature's mouth.

Arky dragged himself forwards. The tunnel didn't get smaller and he realised Jose had lied, but he soon understood why. There was a weird hissing, as though a snake was nearby, or as if the serpent-headed god he was crawling into was alive. It made the hairs on his neck rise and it must have panicked Jose who, like all Suarez's men, was terrified of ghosts.

Arky found it difficult to breathe in the ancient, hot passageway. He took a minute to take a few deep breaths to stop his fears. *The hissing is just air squeezing through the stone somewhere*, he told himself. 'Pezaro crawled in here five hundred years ago,' he said aloud. 'If he could do it, so can I.' His voice echoed in the darkness.

After a metre of wriggling, Arky found himself in a cave-like hollow, obviously the statue's tummy. He felt around till he touched something smooth, about forty centimetres long and thirty deep. He could feel shapes carved into the object's surface.

He put one arm around his find and, using his other hand, he shoved himself back in the direction he had come. Dragging a heavy box backwards was much harder than slithering inside, and sweat poured down Arky's face.

Once he reached the demon's mouth and the light, he could see he was holding a pale green jade chest, heavily engraved with birds and animals.

'Hand it down!' came Suarez's voice.

Arky peered down at the waiting group, as Jose climbed onto Domingo's shoulders and put his hands out for the box. Arky carefully tipped the artefact towards Jose, lowering it slightly. Jose clasped it with both hands and was lifted to the ground by Domingo.

As Jose put the ancient sorcerer's box of secrets on the ground, Domingo pushed Jose away, bent over and pulled up the lid.

'Don't!' Doc shouted, but Domingo was already rummaging inside. He yelped as if bitten and jumped back, wailing in pain. He lifted his hand, revealing a black spike protruding from his palm. A mummified human heart was attached to the other end of the barb. Seeing the gruesome object, the other bandits leapt away, muttering amongst themselves.

'He's cursed!' Pancho cried.

'Can we help him?' Bear asked.

Alice nodded and removed her shirt, wrapping her hand in it. She approached Domingo, who was now pale with fright. 'Sit still,' she ordered. He obeyed her as she pulled the sorcerer's fetish from his hand.

'He's got a deep puncture wound,' she told Suarez, shuddering slightly at the evil-looking human heart.

'This box was an evil sorcerer's possession,' Doc told everyone. 'I think the heart was preserved with a terrible venom. The spike looks like it is made from obsidian.'

'What will happen to me?' cried Domingo.

'You will probably die,' Pancho said.

'You might not,' Doc said quickly. 'The poison is very old.' He turned to Suarez. 'If he gets sick I suggest you send him out of the jungle for medical help.'

Suarez glared at Domingo. 'You are a stupid greedy man,' he growled. 'You deserve to die.'

'Can I come down now?' asked Arky, hopefully. He had clambered to the top of the statue, glad to be away from the sorcerer's poisoned fetish.

Startled by the voice from above, everyone stared up.

'Arky, do you think you can go back inside? I want you to look for the knife,' Doc called up.

'I can't see a thing in there,' said Arky. The thought of going back into the passage seemed more frightening now he'd seen the horrible booby-trap at work. He knew the knife might be needed later to open some sort of gate or pathway, but even so . . .

'I'm sorry,' Doc said, 'but do you think you can try?'

Arky sighed. He knew his dad would never ask unless it was really important. He slid down to the mouth and felt his way forward into the darkness again. When he got to the hollow where the box had been, he felt around carefully. It didn't take him long to touch a smooth shape lying on the stone floor. He withdrew his hand in case the knife was booby-trapped and then reached out slowly again. The sacrificial knife was small but his fingers found a very sharp edge. He clasped the intricate handle, returned quickly, and Doc and Pancho lifted him down.

He held the blade out to his father.

'What is this?' Suarez eyed off the dark knife.

'King Huemac's sorcerer's knife,' Doc said, taking the weapon. 'It cut the hearts out of hundreds of sacrificial victims.'

'Then I will take it!' Suarez grabbed the knife. 'It's not for you to carry weapons! Now—you open the box!' Everyone else stood well back while Doc carefully opened the lid of the jade box with the tip of a stick. Arky held his breath, hoping there were no more booby traps. Inside were feathers and rattles, small carvings and a weird roll of what appeared to be vellum, or calfskin. Doc carefully picked the skin up and unrolled it. It was tattooed with strange hieroglyphics. Doc and Pancho studied them for several minutes. 'The glyphs are Toltec,' Pancho said. 'But they don't make sense. It's not a map and I don't see a city on it at all.'

Doc looked oddly at Pancho and Arky could tell his father understood the map and Pancho didn't. Pancho's knowledge of his own country's history was very poor, Arky thought, especially for a student of archaeology.

'The skin is human,' Doc said, studying the map. 'King Huemac's sorcerers were famous for wearing human skins and using them as talismans. They were known to tattoo messages on them too.'

'Who was King Huemac?' Mia asked.

'King Huemac was not the sort of king we'd like to know,' Doc said. 'He killed hundreds of his people in terrible ceremonies and fought with the Aztecs. An evil sorcerer was his right-hand man. King Huemac was so bad that many people plotted to kill him, but his cunning sorcerer found out about their plans. According to legend, he magically hypnotised them with the beat of his sorcerer's drum, forcing them to dance to its rhythm until they fell over a cliff into the jungle far below, where they were turned into stone.

'Then, still angry with the rest of the people in the city, the sorcerer prayed to the nearby watching volcano and caused it to erupt. Grisly ghosts appeared amongst the flames and they threatened everyone with terrible howls and shrieks.' Suarez's men shifted uncomfortably.

'The people were so frightened they obeyed King Huemac and did his evil bidding without question from that time onwards. When the king died, his son covered his father in jade and put him in a beautiful room filled with gold.'

'And that is what we are looking for,' Suarez said, sounding excited.

Doc lowered his voice for full effect. 'Legend has it that the terrible sorcerer's ghost still guards the city and will attack anyone who threatens the king.'

'And that evil box,' Mia cried, pointing to the jade artefact, 'used to belong to the sorcerer!'

Suarez's men all took a step back from the box. Domingo was slumped against a nearby tree, moaning—a testament to the box's evil powers.

'It's just a legend!' Suarez said. 'Stop trying to scare everyone!'

'This legend helped me find this place where we stand now,' Doc said.

'How?' Bear asked.

'I looked for a threatening, watching volcano.' Doc pointed to the volcano above. 'The volcano has twin vents that look like menacing eyes. There are many huge boulders and rocks lying on the ground under this cliff. With satellite imaging I could see breaks in the jungle where giant rocks had fallen, like hundreds of fallen people, and I could see a large cliff. It all fits with the legend. I couldn't see the city though. It must be well hidden, somewhere above us.'

'So what does this skin show us?' Suarez said. 'Where do we go from here?'

'If it was my expedition, I would go back now,' Doc said. 'Then we would come back here in a week or two with more supplies. I suggest you do that too.'

'We will not go back!' Suarez shouted, pointing the sorcerer's knife. 'We will find this city or you will die looking.' He stepped menacingly towards Alice.

Doc put a protective arm around his wife.

'What do those Toltec marks say? How far do we have to go?' Suarez said.

Doc studied the tattooed skin, then stared up at the volcano. 'The first symbol is for flight. We must start by this jaguar and find a way to go up into the air . . .'

Arky tried to imagine how that would be possible.

'Then when we go up, it looks like we go eight thousand steps towards the eyes of the volcano.' Doc folded the map up. 'But it is too late to start today. I suggest we return to camp, look after Domingo, pack up and tomorrow find our way up the cliff in front of us, which is what I think the symbols mean. Then, as we go, we need to look for flowers that will lead us to the next symbol on the map—the Guardian of the Underworld, a terrible monster.'

Angry Volcano

'There is a ghost behind me,' wailed Domingo, who had been banished to sit with the farting men. 'See him with his black knife!'

The volcano behind them boomed ominously, rocking the ground.

Mia, deciding she could help frighten everyone, screamed convincingly. 'The terrible sorcerer!' she cried.

'You should never have told that sorcerer story!' Jose shouted, looking fearfully around at the shadows cast by the firelight.

'Domingo is feverish,' Alice said, wrapping her arms around Mia, and winking at her. 'And Mia is very susceptible to ghosts. Domingo may be getting tetanus. It is what happens if you get a deep puncture from a dirty nail. Modern medicine could quickly make him better. It is not a curse!'

'Well, he's setting off the others,' Suarez said. 'Find a way to stop it.'

'Send them back,' suggested Pancho. 'We are short of supplies and they are the problem, not us. If Domingo goes, his ghost goes with him.'

Suarez ran his finger over the sharp edge of his machete. 'We go on!'

Squinty and Scarface groaned loudly, gripped their stomachs and let out a foul smell that wafted over to Suarez. He coughed. 'Perhaps I will send them back in the morning,' he said.

The two farting men led Domingo across the river before everyone else had breakfast.

'Now there are only nine men,' Pancho said under his breath. His eyes flickered angrily.

When the camp was packed up, and Suarez had buried the jade box so he could collect it later, everyone returned to the serpent-headed jaguar statue.

Doc, who carried the sorcerer's drawing in his pack, surveyed the landscape.

'So where do we go?' asked Pancho.

'Up towards the volcano,' Doc said, pointing to the cliff. 'The way is hidden because the people in the city were probably kept like prisoners. Only favoured hunters, warriors, priests and nobles would have been able to leave the city through the secret pathway. Maybe they were even blindfolded and led out by the priests. I suspect only the priests knew the way, which is why they were so powerful.'

'You said we had to look for flowers,' Arky said. 'What sort of flowers?'

'See here on the drawing?' Doc held the tattooed human skin out for Arky and Bear to see. 'There are several flowers with a distinct shape and the symbol for eight thousand. These flowers are special symbols for the god Tlaloc, a goggle-eyed god with fangs, who is associated with caves and mountain-top sacrifices. His victims were covered in feathers and flowers before they were killed. Their hearts were torn out, they were skinned and then their bodies were thrown into volcanoes. Their skins were placed in caverns.'

'These people were terrifying,' cried Bear.

'You'd think flowers could be nice,' Mia said quietly.

Doc pointed to the sorcerer's drawing again. 'Then there is another symbol, which represents the God of the Underworld. We should find it in eight thousand steps if we go the right way. All we need to do is work out the first symbol—to fly upwards.'

'Up the cliff in front of us somehow,' Arky said, thinking aloud. 'Perhaps people were hauled up the cliff, or there was a rope hanging down in those days.'

'Good idea.' Alice surveyed the mountain and cliff in front of them. Her expertise in mountain climbing meant she had an excellent eye for finding ways through difficult terrain. 'There is a smooth area at the top of the cliff over there.' She pointed up the rock face several metres above their heads. 'There may have been a rope hanging down once, where people could climb up. If you compare that area with the stone around it, you can see it has suffered years of wear sometime in the past.'

'How do we get up the cliff to get there?' asked Suarez, eyeing the cliff.

'It looks pretty easy,' Arky said. 'Easier than the climbing wall at the gym.'

'We'll go up together then.' Alice smiled at Arky. 'We can lower a rope and haul you up,' she said to Suarez.

Alice and Arky made short work of the cliff and were soon on top. While Alice lowered a rope and hauled up Jose, who was the smallest of Suarez's men, Arky studied the land that lay in front of them. A pathway chipped into stone wound dangerously up a precipitous slope and onwards towards jagged hills, blackened and scorched by many volcanic eruptions. The red-eyed volcano smouldered angrily above it all. An occasional band of green brightened several valleys that had escaped the volcano's fiery attacks. Arky wondered if one of those valleys held the lost city of King Huemac, or if they were too late and the city had long ago been destroyed by the volcano.

As Suarez was hauled up to the track, the volcano burped. The air shook as a dirty cloud of smoke darkened the sky. The noise was almost human, and Arky understood why the people of old thought the volcano was alive.

Bear was much quicker at coming up the cliff than many of Suarez's men and he looked pleased with himself. Arky admired the way Mia kept pushing on too, even though she was only little.

When everyone was assembled, they wound their way along the hazardous path.

'I don't see any carved flowers,' Arky said, after several hundred steps. 'Are we in the right place?'

'There's no other track,' Doc said, but he looked worried. Ahead, the track became narrower and the slope beside it dropped away even more dangerously. Everyone flattened their bodies against the rock wall beside them and sidled forwards. Arky knew a fall here could be fatal and he and Bear moved slowly.

As he crept along behind Pancho, the volcano above them suddenly spewed lava and its red-eyed vents leaked molten tears. The track beneath their feet shook and small stones showered down.

'The track could collapse!' Pancho yelled.

The bandits panicked and began calling out and pushing each other, as larger stones rained down from above, clipping shoulders and thudding onto their packs.

In the pandemonium, while everyone was trying to keep a foothold on the track and duck flying stones, Pancho seized the bandit in front of him and pushed him towards the edge. But the man dug his feet in, turned and grasped Pancho. Struggling fiercely, both men swayed on the convulsing track. Arky leant away to avoid being pulled over with them. Then a stone hurtled down from above, struck Pancho and knocked him over. Still clutching his victim, he tumbled screaming over the edge.

At the same time, Bear, who was still behind Arky on the narrow track, was hit on the shoulder by a rock. It knocked him off-balance. 'Help!' he cried, as he lost his foothold.

Arky, pale with the shock of seeing Pancho's foolish attack, turned at Bear's cry. More stones tumbled towards them and, to Arky's horror, Bear was hit on the chest by several missiles. As he toppled towards the edge, Arky reached out wildly. He managed to grab Bear's arm as his friend went over.

Arky dug his feet into the shaking track and tried to pull Bear to safety. But the volcano hadn't finished: it boomed loudly and the path gave way under Arky's feet. Several rocks whacked into his backpack. He teetered for a moment, fighting gravity, but Bear's weight was dragging him and suddenly they were both tumbling down the slope.

Luckily a loose strap on Arky's backpack caught a jutting rock. It slowed his fall and, with his expertise in rock climbing, he managed to turn and cling to the jagged rock. Bear had caught Arky's feet and came to a halt too.

As quickly as the tremor had started, it stopped. The skittering and sliding rocks ceased falling and Arky could hear Bear's panicked breathing. He lifted his head and looked back up at the track. It was a long way to climb and with Bear hanging on, climbing wasn't an option. He didn't want to look down.

The worried faces of his parents soon appeared over the edge of the track above. 'Hold on, Arky!'

Alice's voice floated down to him over the noise of the growling volcano. 'There is a big drop behind you. I'm coming to get you. Hang on!'

Arky wished his mother hadn't said there was a big drop. Bear's weight was dragging at him. 'Bear,' he said, trying to stay calm. 'Can you dig your feet into something and take a bit of your weight off me? Or can you scramble up me and hang on to this rock?'

'I'm very scared,' whimpered Bear, 'and my shoulder hurts.'

'Well, you might hurt a bit more if you don't try and I slip off this rock.'

To Arky's relief, Bear's weight lightened a little as Bear found a foothold. Then Arky had to grit his teeth as Bear used him as a ladder and climbed over his back.

When his friend was beside him, pale and shaking, Bear latched hold of the rock and was no longer a burden. Safe for the moment, Arky looked around. His eyes quickly met those of Pancho, who was clinging to another rock only metres away.

Behind him was the severe drop that Alice had warned him about.

Suddenly, a well-directed rock bounced down the slope and hit Pancho. Another smacked into his leg, causing him to yell in pain. That one was followed by another that glanced off his head. Blood poured down his face. Arky looked up to see that the bandit Pancho had attacked had managed to scramble to safety and was screaming abuse and hurling stones at his enemy.

Doc, realising the angry bandit was trying to kill Pancho, managed to grab him and stop the stones.

Alice threw down a rope. It uncoiled but fell short of Arky and Bear by several metres. She shimmied down the rope and studied the terrain between the end of the rope and Arky's and Bear's spot. 'I'm coming to get Bear first,' she said, realising Bear could not hold on as long as Arky.

Alice's expert fingers quickly found small cracks and folds in the rock and she made her way towards Bear. First she removed their backpacks so the bags wouldn't upset their balance.

The packs slithered and bounced away, plunging into oblivion. Then she manoeuvred herself behind Bear. 'Bear,' she soothed, 'in front of you is a deep crack. I've got my shoulders right behind your feet. So I want you to stand on my shoulders, then push up and grab hold of that crack.'

Bear took a deep breath and did as he was told.

'Well done!' cried Arky and Alice together, as Bear found the grip and hauled himself higher. Alice then used one hand to place Bear's toes on a fold in the rock. 'Now push up again! There's another handhold not far away.

'I will come back for you.' Alice smiled reassuringly at Arky as she laboured up the cliff with Bear.

'I can do it on my own,' Arky said, watching them.

'It is safer if you wait,' Alice said, helping Bear to climb the few metres to the hanging rope.

'Help!' Pancho cried, his eyes wide with fear. 'I can't hold on much longer!' He looked exhausted and his eyes pleaded with Arky.

Alice was concentrating on helping Bear up the rope. Arky knew it would be several minutes before she could return. Pancho's knuckles were white and his arms were shaking with strain. He could fall to his doom at any minute. Arky had to help. *If I could get over to him and remove his pack, like Mum did with us,* thought Arky, *Pancho could hold on till help comes.*

As Pancho was so close, Arky decided to make a move. Bravely, he reached out until his fingers found a hold and he swivelled sideways, crabbing his way to Pancho's side. 'I'm going to release your pack,' he told Pancho, 'so you won't have so much weight on you.' Arky pushed his hand under Pancho's stomach and unclipped the pack's straps. It fell away.

Pancho drew a deep breath and his eyes filled with gratitude.

Arky looked down at Pancho's left foot. It was several centimetres below a crack. 'Move your foot up a little,' instructed Arky. 'You will feel a crevice. Stick your toe in it. This will help hold you till Mum can get here.'

Shaking, Pancho did as he was told and a wave of relief flooded his face. 'I owe you,' he said rather gruffly.

Relieved, Arky looked up. Bear had just reached the track and was being helped to Doc's side. The rope was re-lowered and Alice quickly joined Arky and Pancho. It didn't take long for Arky and Alice to help Pancho climb to safety.

Suarez was not happy to see Pancho clamber to safety. As punishment for trying to murder one of his men, Suarez tied Pancho's hands behind his back. 'If you trip and fall I won't let anyone save you again,' Suarez hissed. 'If you cause one more bit of trouble I'll shoot you!' He was about to launch into more threats when Arky noticed an odd design in the rocks behind Suarez's head.

He pointed. 'A flower!'

Suarez turned. Sure enough, faded with age and almost obliterated by rock falls, a flower was chipped into the rock. The mood of the group suddenly lightened and they moved forwards expectantly.

Further on, the track forked and Bear was the first to sight another flower pointing the way. The bandits hurried ahead and, within minutes, the track became wider and safer so everyone could move easily.

Guardian of
the Underworld

Later in the day, as the flowers led them through gullies and over hills, they came to a narrow valley. It wound around a sharp bend, and ended in front of a huge cliff. Carved into the towering walls was a terrifying statue.

'The Guardian of the Underworld!' Doc cried excitedly, running over to explore the carving. 'Xolotl!'

The Guardian of the Underworld emerged from the living rock. He was three metres high. Ghosts of the ancients shone from the guardian's glittering obsidian eyes, which were set into a skull-like head.

The head sported a fan-like headdress and large ear spools held human bones. A carved necklace of human eyeballs hung from his neck. Xolotl's hungry mouth looked like it was waiting to swallow anyone walking past and his arms were raised as if he wanted to rip the explorers apart. Mystic, chilling and enchanting—the statue took Arky's breath away.

'It's a dead-end.' Suarez stared at the towering walls around them. 'You have led us nowhere!'

'No!' cried Pancho, sitting down as if he was in shock. 'It can't be.'

'Dead-end!' Bear sniggered, looking up at the skeletal god.

'There has to be a way forward.' Mia stared hard at the rock.

'The knife,' Arky reminded Doc. 'The sorcerer's knife!'

Doc smiled. 'Of course! Pezaro said he left the knife to *open the way*. I want everyone to study the guardian statue and see if there is a slit or a keyhole anywhere that might open a doorway or secret entrance. Perhaps it will lead us to a cave in the cliff.'

At Doc's words, Suarez took the obsidian knife from his backpack and, waving it dangerously, rushed forwards with his men. They started patting and inspecting every inch of the guardian statue and arguing about where a keyhole might be found.

Arky, Bear and Mia were forgotten about and they moved off. There were trees and shrubs growing nearby and Bear sat in the shade to take a rest. Arky could see Bear was still shaken by the fall on the track. Mia, however, seemed restless and she wandered away. Suddenly she started laughing and talking.

Arky shook his head. 'I don't know where she's coming from at times.'

'Listen to her!' Bear smiled. 'She's saying, *You are a handsome man. Will you marry me?* Seriously, girls!'

Arky's curiosity got the better of him. He stood up and went over to see what Mia was doing.

She was up beside the cliff, chatting loudly to a huge, round stone human head, twice her size. The basalt sculpture rested against the cliff. It appeared old and wise, with stiff curls for hair, a curved nose, and wide-open eyes staring gently into space. Its soft lips made it look friendly. Beside the disembodied head was another, almost hidden from sight by bushes and shrubs.

'It is a lonely giant,' Mia said as Arky joined her. 'He is waiting to wake up. Kissy, kissy!' She laughed, giving the statue in front of her a kiss. 'It might wake up and be a prince,' she told Arky. She moved to the next head. 'And this one, it might be hungry, as it has a litle hole in its mouth.'

Arky took one look at the mouth on the strange hidden statue and his heart leapt as an idea came to him. He ran back to Doc. He arrived just in time—the bandits had had no luck searching for a secret doorway and they were grumbling loudly. Suarez was looking murderously at Doc, and Alice had gone rather pale.

'Heads!' shouted Arky. 'Come.'

With everyone following, Arky led the way back to the heads. He pointed to the odd statues. 'One has a little slit in its mouth,' he explained. 'I think the knife would fit inside.'

'But it's so big and round!' Alice was running her hand over the head. 'It can't be the way forward.'

'It could hide a door,' Arky said.

'You're right,' Doc said. 'Xolotl was big on human heads. He founded a game that is a bit like soccer, called the Ulama game. The Toltecs loved this game, but instead of advertising around the edge of the playing field as we do today, they had racks of human skulls. Some say the ball of the Ulama game was originally a human head.' Doc pointed to the large stone heads beside him. 'These heads are round, so they could be symbols of Xolotl's favourite game.'

'Yuck!' Mia cried. 'I kissed it!'

Doc inspected the slit in the head's mouth. 'I need the knife.' He held his hand out and Suarez passed the blade across. 'Perhaps the head moves somehow, and the knife releases a lock.' Doc pushed the sorcerer's knife into the mouth. There was a click and the statue rocked slightly. 'It sounds like something dropped down inside,' Doc said, handing the knife back to Suarez.

'Perhaps we have to push it,' Arky suggested.

'Look!' Bear pointed to the ground. 'I think I can see where something like little wheels might have worn away the rock. Dirt and plants have gathered in it.'

'You're right!' Doc fell to his knees and pulled the plants away. Soon he'd uncovered well-worn, almost polished, stone tracks.

'It looks like ball bearings have gone over it,' Arky said. 'The knife must have released a lock and some sort of wheels have dropped down.'

'Push!' ordered Suarez. 'Don't talk. Push.'

Everyone leant their shoulders on the heavy stone head and strained against it. Slowly, with a grinding scream, the head moved along the ancient path. As it crept away from the cliff a terrible smell wafted through the air, and a dark reeking cavern was revealed.

'The opening to the underworld, the haunt of the god Xolotl,' Doc said as they all peered into the darkness.

❖

Meanwhile, Skull-head and his henchmen were standing beside the serpent-headed jaguar in the jungle. Skull-head was inspecting a tree with an arrow mark hacked into its bark. The arrow pointed to the sky. 'Here's another one.' He smiled. 'They have gone up that cliff.' He turned to one of his henchmen. 'Unpack Suarez's stinking donkeys. Then bring me a rope. We'll have to get up there and follow them.'

The other man ambled over to Squinty, Scarface and Domingo, who they had captured. The trio was heavily laden with the other gang's camping equipment. The man avoided the two stinking men and went to Domingo, who seemed to have recovered from his injury. Domingo glared as his pack was removed, and a rope found.

Skull-head turned to his prisoners. 'We have to climb the cliff. You are too much trouble. We will tie you to the trees.' An enormous fart from Squinty drowned out his words. Skull-head and his men shuddered. 'Your stink should frighten off even the wildest animals, so you will be here to help us carry back the treasure we take from your idiot boss!'

Deathly Surrounds

'Before we go into this cavern—' Doc peered into the putrid hole, '—I want you to know I suspect it will not be a straightforward journey. To help us through, I think you need to understand the legend of Xolotl.'

'No more stories!' shouted Suarez and several of his men at the same time.

'But the stories might save your lives,' insisted Doc. 'Xolotl was the god of bad luck, and it would be bad luck to go inside without knowing a little about him.' Doc held up the terrible sorcerer's skin. 'Here there are symbols of bats and spiders. These animals were sacred to Xolotl, as was the eleventh hour of the day. He also used human bones to frighten people escaping from the underworld. He would not make a journey through darkness easy for anyone entering his realm. I think we will find many dead-ends or mazes inside. I should also warn you that many of his victims' bodies were placed in caves.'

'It is the smell of the dead inside!' Jose cried, interrupting Doc's story. 'It is bad luck to go on. Their ghosts will haunt us.'

Suarez turned on Jose. 'If you don't shut up, you will be the first to go inside.'

'But I don't want to go on!' Jose said. 'Let me stay here.'

'I do not like arguing!' Suarez said viciously. 'You are a small man, but you are the only one who can stand upright in that hole. You can lead us.' He pointed to Arky and Bear. 'In fact, you are such a big baby, we will send the children with you, and then Doctor Steele can follow. You won't be able to run away with us all behind you.' Suarez pushed Jose to the front of the group. 'We go in now!' He turned and glared at Doc. 'You figure the clues out and say nothing more!'

'Can you untie my hands?' Pancho called out. 'I will never be able to walk in there so bent, with my hands tied as well.'

Suarez nodded and cut Pancho's bonds. 'You will be in front of me so there are no tricks,' he warned, holding up the obsidian knife.

When everyone had retrieved their torches, Jose, his face as pale as a ghost and his hands shaking, took the first step into the gloom.

The smell made Arky nauseous. He put his fingers over his nose and followed Jose. Bear and Mia did the same. Their torch beams reflected bright stone chips in the walls, glittering like diamonds. If it weren't for the smell, it would have been beautiful.

'What's twinkling on the walls?' Bear asked, his voice reverberating eerily in the confined space.

'Mica and obsidian,' Doc said from behind. 'I think this is an old lava chimney that has been carved out by humans in later times.'

The ancient volcano vent opened out eventually and, relieved, the adults stood upright. Further on into the darkness the tunnel became a cavern, stuffy and spooky. Arky slipped on something black and slimy. The ooze became thicker with every step. The smell also increased till he wanted to vomit. 'What's that smell?' He gagged as his feet squelched in the stinking goo.

'It is poo!' yelled Mia. 'My feet are in poo and it is coming in over my shoes!'

'Bats,' said Alice. 'It comes from bats.'

'What sort of bats?' Bear shone his torch upwards at hundreds of flapping creatures. As the light hit them they fluttered angrily and erupted from their perches, twittering, flapping and swooping around the intruders.

'Vampires!' screamed one of the bandits as one flew at his head. His shout startled the distressed bats even more and poo rained down on everyone.

'They'll suck your blood!' screamed another bandit.

'And give you rabies!' shouted Pancho, adding to the uproar.

Horrified, everyone started trying to dodge the poo. Arky and Bear were jostled on all sides. As a large glob of poo slid down Arky's neck, his torch lit a crevice. Thinking it might be a good place to hide from the bombs, he pulled Bear inside. As bats swooped and everyone screamed and squealed, Bear shone his torch further down the opening behind them. He thought he saw something glimmer. Curious, he pushed past Arky to investigate. He stepped into a small room, and came face to face with a large-fanged, blood-splattered, open-mouthed, demonic face. Other ferocious masks glared down from a rack above his head.

'They're probably the sorcerer's masks,' Arky said, chilled by the horrible faces. 'He might have used them to frighten people. Let's get out of here in case they're booby-trapped like his other stuff.'

Bear needed no further warning and he twisted around to return. But his shoes, slippery with bat poo, went out from under him. He crashed heavily backwards into the rack of masks. The gruesome faces tumbled down with a clatter. One of the masks landed firmly on Bear's head. 'Get it off!' he screamed, trying to pull off the disgusting artefact. But something inside the mask was stuck in his hair and, as he pulled, it hurt. What if it was another of those obsidian spikes, dripping venom? Bear panicked and, with a shattering cry, dashed back into the main tunnel with Arky hot on his heels.

The sight of a heavily-fanged shrieking monster, emerging from what appeared to be the living rock, was too much for poor Jose. He let out a blood-curdling screech and ran for his life.

By the time Arky got to Bear's side and Alice and Doc arrived to help, the bandits were down another man.

Doc removed the ancient facemask from Bear's head and showed Bear an old clip that would have once helped secure the mask to the sorcerer's head. The bats were still bombing everyone so Suarez hurriedly ordered the group forwards.

The tunnel kept going straight ahead. Arky began to think the way through the mountain was easy and that Doc had been wrong about there being a possible maze, when the tunnel suddenly forked into three passageways.

'Which way?' Suarez asked.

'That way.' Arky pointed, his sharp eyes drawn to a painting on the wall. 'See, there is a spider on the wall of that tunnel.' He remembered what Doc had said about the spider being sacred to Xolotl.

'Well spotted,' Doc said. 'We go down the spider tunnel.'

'I hope there are no spiders.' Alice shivered.

The spider tunnel was so narrow everyone had to walk single file for several minutes, until it suddenly opened into an enormous cavern. The bats in this cavern fluttered on the ceiling, but as they were so far above the intruders they didn't feel threatened and stayed put.

Arky and Bear shone their torches over the walls and found many smaller tunnels leading in different directions.

'How do we know where to go now?' Suarez asked, looking dismayed.

Arky realised Doc's legend would be the clue. He began counting the passageways that lay before them. 'Fourteen,' he said. 'There are fourteen passages.'

'So, which one would you choose?' Doc looked encouragingly at Arky.

'You said that eleven was the sacred number for the God of the Underworld,' Arky said. 'So, I would choose the eleventh passage. But which way do we count? From the right or from the left?'

'I'd go the way of the sun rising,' Bear said, inspired by Arky's thinking. 'As the eleventh hour belongs to Xolotl, I'd choose the eleventh tunnel from the east side. As that is the way the sun comes up and you'd follow the sun across the sky from east to west!'

'Well done, Bear!' Doc smiled.

'You boys are brilliant!' Alice looked at them admiringly. 'I'd never have thought of it like that!'

Doc studied his GPS and stepped towards the chosen tunnel.

'The eleventh hour,' Alice said, as they went into the tunnel. 'There is a saying—*at the eleventh hour we were saved*—it's like saying we were saved in the nick of time. I wonder if that saying came from the legend of Xolotl?'

'Maybe at the eleventh hour we'll get our revenge on Suarez,' muttered Pancho, emerging from behind everyone.

To everyone's relief the eleventh tunnel opened out into light just on dusk. The setting sun showed they had arrived on a wide ledge beside a deep valley.

The last rays of light also shone on hundreds of human skulls placed in small caves carved into the cliff. It was a terrifying sight and Arky realised that only the bravest warrior would have dared to enter the cavern of Xolotl, even if they were trying to escape from King Huemac's hidden valley.

Shuddering, Arky turned his back on the bones and walked to the escarpment to study the valley below. The misty, narrow gorge was heavily shadowed by the volcano, but even in the dying light Arky could see the heads of towering trees.

'Thanks to you, Arky,' Doc said, coming to stand beside his son, 'we have found our way to the hidden city.'

'The track ahead is narrow,' Alice said, 'and I wouldn't like to go down into the valley in the dark.'

Suarez nervously looked over his shoulder at the skulls and then peered down the darkened track. Arky noticed the bandit leader couldn't make up his mind whether to risk an unknown track or camp beside the creepy skulls.

'There could be booby-traps on the path,' Arky said. 'After all, it is the sorcerer's secret pathway.'

'We camp here then,' Suarez said quickly.

When they lit their fires, the bats erupted from the cavern. Thousands of the creatures flapped past Arky, Bear and the others, creating eerie shapes against the moon. Overhead the towering, evil-eyed volcano belched and roared. The molten lava lit the night sky with a bloody hue.

Mia looked as unhappy as Arky felt. She snuggled up with Alice for comfort, and Doc wrapped his arms around Arky and Bear. Eventually, Suarez handed out the evening meal. Because they were so low on supplies, he didn't give much to the prisoners.

Arky's stomach was complaining and he was about to leap upon his tiny meal, when he noticed

Pancho hadn't been given anything at all. Suarez and the bandits were still furious with him for trying to kill their man. Doc, Alice, Bear and Mia stopped eating as Arky handed Pancho some of his dinner. Doc quickly made sure Pancho had an equal share of their food. Pancho nodded his thanks but he sat apart from the others, avoiding their eyes.

In the morning, breakfast was not on offer and Suarez ordered an early start. They moved down the track into the valley. Bear's stomach was rumbling in time with the volcano.

At the bottom of the track they found themselves in an ancient forest. The trees were enormous, growing tall to catch the meagre light sneaking around the roaring volcano's shadow.

As they walked, Arky noticed a pottery jar, about the height of his hip, lying beneath the root of a tree. Then more jars appeared. Some were almost overgrown by plants, while others looked as if they had only been placed on the ground yesterday. The army of pottery pygmies was rather unsettling.

'What are they?' Arky asked.

'The Toltecs put the ashes of their dead in those jars, and sometimes their treasured possessions,' Doc said. 'We must be getting close to the city.'

One of the bandits overheard Doc. He stopped beside one of the urns and peered inside. 'Gold!' he called out. 'There is gold inside them!' Greedily, he thrust his hand into the jar. Just as quickly, he recoiled, clutching a golden bracelet. His face was white with shock, and his agonised groan alerted everyone to trouble.

Before anyone could help him, the bandit fell to the ground. Behind him, from the mouth of the jar, a long pinkish snake with brown scaly squares on its body slithered away.

'Bushmaster,' breathed Mia. 'He has been bitten by a bushmaster.'

Alice and Doc rushed to the bandit's side to see if they could help. The man's hand, now paralysed, had deep, bleeding puncture wounds. To Arky's horror, as the bandit's teeth chattered uncontrollably, his skin turned a luminous yellow-green. Seconds later, he fell silent and breathed no more, still clutching his golden bracelet.

'He's dead,' Pancho said.

Doc pulled Arky and Bear away. 'There is nothing anyone can do. Death occurs quickly from a bushmaster.'

'Seven men left,' Pancho whispered, nudging Doc happily.

After the encounter with Bear in the facemask, Jose ran from the cavern as if a thousand ghosts were after him. His one thought was to escape the demons and get back to civilisation. When he reached the light and emerged near the stone head, he took off down the track and kept going. Past the flowers and along the cliff track he ran, retracing his steps.

Exhausted and puffing, he rounded a corner and ran headlong into Skull-head, who was studying a fork in the trail. Skull-head drew his gun.

'How fortunate,' he said. 'We were just wondering which way to go and here you are to show us!'

The Jade-encrusted King

Depression descended on the group after the bushmaster attack. Several bandits muttered amongst themselves and Mia told Arky they were using words like 'doomed' and 'cursed'. To make matters worse, a fine ash had spewed from the hissing volcano. Occasionally, a cinder got inside Arky's nose or irritated his eyes.

Alice ripped up some clothes and made bandanas. She made everyone tie them around their heads, covering their mouth and nose. Arky found it a little easier to breathe.

'Have you noticed that Pancho is the only one who seems happy?' Bear asked quietly. 'I mean, since the bushmaster attack, he's been beaming.'

'I guess he thinks we can escape Suarez,' Arky said. 'Though I don't like him like I used to.'

'Me neither,' Bear said. 'When there is trouble your real personality comes out. I get the feeling he's only looking out for himself.'

'Not like Mia.' Arky smiled, with a flare of admiration for their solid little companion. 'Who'd have thought she'd be so amazing?'

'And your mum!' Bear said. 'I knew she was a kick-arse mountaineer, but I never knew how brave she really was. Wait till my mum hears about how she saved me on that cliff. My mum will want someone to write a film about our adventure.'

'And she'll want to play Alice!' Arky laughed at the thought of Bear's mum, Linda Redford, playing his mum.

The boys were so engrossed in their chatter that Arky's usually sharp eyes didn't see the first building, but the next one stopped everyone in their tracks. It was built, stone upon stone, up the side of the cliff. Its narrow slit windows were covered in vines and creepers.

'It's real.' Doc sucked his breath in and rocked excitedly on his feet.

Alice, her eyes alight with excitement, gripped Doc's hand. 'We've found the lost city!'

Bear and Arky walked over to the building and looked in through the eerily silent, leaf-littered doorway. Bones scattered on a once-tiled floor told of the many people who must have lived inside.

'The speckled fever must have killed them,' Arky said. 'They've just fallen to the ground and no one's moved them.'

'What disease do you think they died from?' Bear asked Doc, who had come up beside them with Alice and Mia.

'I suspect Pezaro and Francisco might have brought either smallpox or measles with them,' Doc said. 'The native inhabitants weren't immune to those diseases. Smallpox killed almost every child and was eighty to ninety per cent fatal in adults in Central America. Measles also wiped out whole populations.' Doc looked sadly around the empty building. 'I suppose, even if some adults lived afterwards, the children would have all been dead and the way out of this valley was hidden and—'

His last words were lost as a massive blast shook the volcano and reverberated through the valley. More black ash fell from the sky and a dark cloud loomed overhead.

'I don't like this at all,' Alice said, dusting cinders from her hair. 'I think we might be about to have a full-scale eruption. I don't want to be here if that happens.'

'Look!' Mia pointed to the slope above. 'The eyes are leaking red-hot stone.'

Sure enough, a long stain of lava was winding its way slowly down the slopes above.

'Hurry!' Suarez yelled, seeing his prisoners had fallen behind.

They passed more and more houses as they travelled through narrow streets. Arky wondered what they would find. What would be left of the palace and the king? Eventually, they found themselves in the centre of the ancient city. A ball court, just as Doc had described when they were at the stone heads, lay before them. The rows of stone seats behind the court were decorated with fallen skulls. The court was overgrown with ferns and vines. An imposing pyramid set with steep stairs towered above the court and led to a platform high above their heads. Magnificent snake sculptures, paired in looping lines, led from the court to the pyramid.

Bear pointed at the pyramid. 'It's just like we saw in the books. It's all the things we talked about and wanted to see. That's the pyramid of the sun, where the priests cut out the hearts of their victims!' He turned to Doc. 'It's better than any Aztec ruin. How many people do you think the Toltecs slaughtered here?'

'And there's the palace,' Alice said, changing the gruesome subject. 'It's just behind the pyramid. You can see the courtyard and its columns.'

Behind them, Arky noticed Suarez was casting worried glances at the threatening volcano. He almost ran to the three-storey palace.

Arky eyed the ancient building. The roof had long collapsed and stone columns had been knocked to the ground, possibly by earthquakes, but the first two floors looked easy to enter.

Suarez pushed Arky inside with the others and they passed through a colonnaded front entrance with gilded walls. Next they found a reception room full of wall paintings, carvings and golden panels. Arky was amazed at how much had survived intact over such a long period.

Marble steps led to the second floor and they followed Doc through the rooms to the king's meeting chamber, where a magnificent carved throne, glittering with jewels and pearls, sat empty. Beside the throne lay several skeletons, frozen in death. Their brightly woven clothes still covered their bones. Arky thought they may have been servants because, in some of the passageways, other bodies lay clutching silver plates or beautiful glassware in gnarled hands. It was as if they had died still trying to do their work.

'It's like Sleeping Beauty's castle,' Bear said. 'Except everyone is rotten.'

Mia smiled up at Arky. 'And even though a handsome prince has come to this castle, I don't think he would want to kiss a princess if she looked like that!' She pointed to a skeleton that had fallen beside a window. A large creeper grew through its ribs and leaves sprouted from its eye sockets. A large black spider sat in a web above its head.

'We might get a princess to kiss the Jade-encrusted King,' Arky joked back. 'What would you do if he woke?'

'I might kiss him, if he really is covered in gold.' Mia smiled. 'I could kiss an ugly rich king.'

'Girls!' Bear snorted and shook his head.

'You are rich,' Mia laughed, 'but I wouldn't kiss you!'

Doc had been peering into several sumptuous rooms and now he opened a huge double door. 'The Room of Feathers!' he cried, as a room decorated with brilliant feathers—yellow, radiant blue and sparkling hues of red—opened up before them. 'I can't believe it! I've read about such rooms!' He rushed inside, enjoying a feast for the eyes. Feathers of every kind were woven into tapestries and festooned the walls. A dazzling cloak, decorated in pearls and plumage of the purest and most dazzling white, lay across the back of a gilded chair. The room was joyful and beautiful, and such a contrast to the death and destruction outside.

For once the bandits stood speechless. Before them lay treasures that would provide every man there, and their grandchildren, with wealth beyond their dreams.

'And the king?' Pancho asked. 'Where would we find the king?'

'I think he'd be in the next room,' Doc said, taken aback, as Pancho pushed him aside and eagerly opened another door at the back of the Room of Feathers. Everyone followed.

There before them lay the story as it was written in the Spanish Diary. The room was sumptuous: embroidered tapestries tangled with spider webs hung from the walls. A skeletal body lay on the floor, wearing a plumed headdress and golden waistband, with a necklace of bones and claws around its neck.

'It's the sorcerer,' Bear said, stepping forward to study the body.

Beside the sorcerer, on a bed of gold and ruined linen, lay the blackened remains of the last King Huemac.

Pancho looked around, dismayed. 'I meant the Jade-encrusted King!' he yelled. '*That king* and the room of gold!'

Arky noticed Doc was trying to keep his cool at Pancho's rudeness. There was an angry silence for a minute, as Doc set his jaw. Finally he answered in a slow, polite tone: 'The diary didn't say where the Jade-encrusted King lay, but I think he would be kept close to his descendant. Perhaps there is a secret door.'

'Find it!' Suarez moved up beside Doc and pulled out his gun. 'You and your stories, you must have some idea!'

Seeing Doc threatened, Alice moved up and stood between him and Suarez. Arky, Bear and Mia joined her. 'We will try,' Alice said, her voice gentle and calm against the roar of the volcano outside and the greedy gold fever of the men around her.

'All I know is that the body of the first King Huemac was covered in gold and jade,' Doc said.

'His body was worshipped by his descendants. I don't know anything else about him, or how to find his sacred room.'

Suarez, Pancho and Doc began a heated discussion about what to do next and Arky pulled Bear close and whispered, 'Look! Behind the dead king's bed. See, there is a golden pull cord. It looks like a hangman's noose. Remember how we read about King Huemac hanging himself? That's how he died. I wonder if it is a clue?'

'What do you mean?' Bear asked.

'Maybe like all the symbols Dad has been talking about,' Arky whispered. 'Perhaps the hangman's noose is the symbol of King Huemac's death. The noose might not summon servants or ring a bell. What if it opened a secret door?'

Bear reached up and touched the strange noose. 'It's made of solid twisted gold,' he whispered. 'You're right, Arky. Why would you have a pull cord like this if it only rang a bell?' He gripped the rope and pulled hard.

To Arky's delight the cord moved, and a tapestry

behind the dead king folded in on itself and revealed a golden door.

Before anyone could turn around, Arky leapt towards the door and pushed. It opened with a grinding squeak and a darkened room, like a crypt, was revealed.

There were no windows and only the light from the doorway reflected dully from the golden walls. As his eyes became accustomed to the gloom, Arky saw offerings of jaguar skins, painted ceramics, shells, pearls, mirrors and tiny golden statues surrounding the Jade-encrusted King.

The fabled first King Huemac lay on a marble plinth on a cloth of gold brocade. Golden cups, plates, statues and ingots lay piled around his plinth.

The bandits could not restrain themselves. They fell upon the piles of gold, throwing objects into their packs and squabbling over the finer pieces. The prisoners were ignored and Doc moved forwards to inspect the fabulous mummy.

The partially preserved body of King Huemac was covered with carved jade squares, stitched together with loops of gold, forming a suit. An enormous jade necklace, embossed with pearls, decorated his chest. His head, still with braided hair attached, was adorned with skilfully carved golden feathers. His eyeballs had long gone but, beneath the leathery eyelids, someone had placed white marbles, inlaid with obsidian irises. They glared goggle-eyed from the long empty sockets. The king's blackened lips were set in a frozen frown.

'I don't know how we're going to get this out,' Pancho said. 'We can't carry it.'

'We're not moving it,' Doc said, shocked. 'We won't help Suarez. It can't be moved by hand! If we get out alive, we'll bring the government back and have it preserved and moved carefully.'

'Helicopter then,' Pancho said, ignoring Doc. He seemed to be in a world of his own. 'It will need a helicopter.'

Be Careful What You Wish For

That night, Suarez took his gold-laden bandits out of the palace and made camp on the old playing court. No one wished to sleep inside the palace, as the rumbling from the nearby volcano was causing bricks to fall and the walls to quake.

Suarez forced Doc and Alice to empty their packs of travelling necessities and fill them with gold. He was a happy man and his men sat around a bright fire, laughing and joking and inspecting their brilliant artefacts.

The boys and Pancho, who had lost their packs, were forced to carry golden trinkets in bundles made from the tents. Suarez put golden necklaces and bracelets on Mia's arms and neck, decking her out like a store dummy. 'You can look beautiful while we travel,' he had said, and grinned. 'But you will have to give it back.'

Camping in the playing court was very uncomfortable and Bear started to annoy Arky by grumbling. Even though Arky understood how his friend felt, he wished he'd shut his mouth.

'Ash is falling on us. I'm starving. I wish I had some food.'

'Stop wishing for things that aren't here!' Arky snapped. 'Mia isn't complaining and you shouldn't either.'

'I am complaining on the inside,' Mia said. 'I am very unhappy and I wish I had some food. Suarez is a bad man! I wish he was made to suffer. I wish someone would rob him like he robs others!' She stamped her foot, took off the golden jewellery and threw the pieces on the ground. Then she plonked herself down beside Bear and glared into the darkness.

'Try to sleep,' Alice said, feeling sorry for the children. 'We will have a hard trip tomorrow and we will have to pull together as a team. Use your energy to help each other.'

'I hope Suarez doesn't get his hands on the Jade-encrusted King,' Doc said. 'I wish someone would stop him. He knows nothing of history.'

A little later, as everyone tried to settle to sleep, Arky saw something move in the shadows at the edge of the playing court. He strained his eyes in the gloom. The shape moved again. Arky was sure it was a man. His blood chilled. 'Dad!' He whispered to Doc. 'Could people still be living here?'

'Why?' Doc said.

'I saw something move. Out at the edge of the court.'

'Probably one of Suarez's men going to the toilet,' Doc said. 'I don't think there are any head-hunting Toltecs out there. Go to sleep.'

But Arky couldn't sleep. He tossed and turned. He watched as Doc and Alice fell asleep beside

Mia, and Bear made snuffling sounds through his nose.

The volcanic ash fell faster, covering everyone in a fine blanket. Eventually Arky must have fallen asleep because a bad dream woke him and he sat up, frightened. The campfire was low and the moon shone briefly through a gap in the ash clouds, revealing several shadows moving across the playing court.

Arky rubbed his eyes but, like a nightmare, the shadows had human shapes and were headed towards the embers of Suarez's fire. *I'm not dreaming*, Arky thought, his heart thundering in fear. It took him a second to find his voice. 'Head-hunters!' he screamed. 'We're being attacked!'

His alarm galvanised everyone. The bandits struggled to their feet. Torches flicked on, and the shadows raced towards Suarez's bleary men. A gun was fired and Pancho, who was sleeping several metres away, leapt to his feet and charged headlong into the fray with a mighty roar.

'Keep low!' Alice pulled Arky down as more gunfire echoed across the court. 'They're not watching us. Move backwards on your tummies.'

'Move towards the old houses,' Doc said. 'We might be able to hide in there and escape.'

'You won't hide, Doctor Steele,' said a voice from behind. Arky turned. Doc switched on his torch, lighting the scowling face of Skull-head. He was holding a gun. 'I'm afraid you'll have to sit very still or I will shoot you. You have done your job and are no longer needed. But I will await my orders before I send you off to the underworld.'

Behind them, there was the odd cry as men were injured. Knives flashed in the light of fallen torches and, within minutes, the battle was over. 'We've got them!' came a voice. 'All tied up and with sacks of lovely gold ready to take home!'

Skull-head marched his prisoners over to join Suarez's men. Blood oozed from a wound in Suarez's shoulder. The other bandits sported bruises and wounds but they were all alive. Jose, tied firmly, was dragged forwards from the edge of the court and thrown to the ground in front of Suarez.

'Your little deserter showed us the way.' Skull-head smiled.

Arky looked around for Pancho. He wasn't with Suarez's men. 'I hope Pancho hasn't been killed,' he whispered to Bear.

'He might be hiding.' Bear wiped ash from his face. 'He might try to save us later.'

As he spoke, Pancho ambled up to Skull-head. 'Well done,' he said, shaking his hand. 'I didn't expect you so soon.'

'You made it easy with your marks,' Skull-head replied, 'and thanks to your key helping us out of the truck, we were only delayed a few hours.'

Doc leapt to his feet. 'Pancho!' he cried angrily. 'How could you do this to us! What made you?'

'A lot of money,' Pancho said, and shrugged. He turned back to Skull-head. 'We're hungry. Give me some food.' He pointed to Arky, Bear and Mia, and Doc and Alice. 'They looked after me, so give them some too.'

Surprised, Skull-head did as he was told.

As angry and confused as he was with Pancho, Arky fell upon the food hungrily.

'My wish came true,' Bear said, chewing loudly. 'I've got some food.'

'My wish did too,' Mia said. 'Someone has robbed Suarez.'

'Well,' said Arky, feeling exasperated, 'you should be careful what you wish for from now on. We could be in more trouble than ever!'

In the small hours of the night, the volcano's fiery belly shot forth ash and massive gaseous clouds rolled down the mountain. Huge flashes of forked lightning played on the edge of the vapours, creating an amazing and terrifying spectacle. The volcano's twin eyes changed colour from red to yellow, then orange and purple, as the clouds played in front of them and their hot tears edged ever closer.

Arky and Bear stayed awake watching—both scared and amazed by the volcano's power. No one else slept either. So when the sun rose, and lit the valley with eerie lilac light, everyone was tired and distressed. 'We should get out while we can,' Alice said. 'I think the volcano will blow.'

'It looks very dangerous,' Pancho said. 'But we can fit in a quick trip to the palace. My men will want more treasure. If this place is destroyed, I want it to have paid for my trip.' He quickly checked the bonds tying Suarez's gang together, and led the way back to the palace.

The air had become darker and ash was falling thicker and faster. The ground groaned and stones and bricks from the palace tumbled to the ground around them. 'I will not take the children inside,' Alice said, stopping dead in her tracks before the rocking building.

'Your husband comes with us. Stay if you like,' Pancho said, as a tile bounced down from the roof above. 'We will be as fast as possible.'

When Pancho's bandits disappeared inside, an explosion above sent pebbles of light white stone bursting from the sky. 'Pumice,' Alice said, grabbing Arky and Bear to her. Mia was already holding on. 'We are lucky it's not red-hot! But it is a warning that things will get worse.'

In the thickening clouds, they waited impatiently for Doc to reappear. Slow minutes ticked by, and Arky thought his dad had been gone about half an hour when the sound of a loud rumble like a freight train startled everyone. Bear looked at Arky, wide-eyed. Suddenly, the earth convulsed. It wasn't like the little shakes they had experienced previously. This time the ground moved like a wave, rolling towards them and throwing them from their feet. Arky's body slammed against the dirt. A huge crack split the road beside them. Gas hissed from the bowels of the earth.

Arky and Alice quickly found their feet and helped Bear and Mia to stand. Just then, Doc stumbled from the palace in a cloud of dust. The ground trembled again and Doc, with his heavy pack, was thrown down the stairs. A column collapsed beside him, bringing down part of the palace above. It just missed Doc and Arky ran towards him to help him up.

Pancho appeared next and was tossed sideways. He rolled down the stone steps and his men staggered behind him. The bouncing palace groaned and bricks and tiles fell clattering to the earth. Everything lurched and rocked back and forth, and the ground underfoot roared in agony as it was bent and torn.

When the quake ended, most of the palace had collapsed. A crack had formed right through the centre of the building, splitting it in two. Worse, ash from the volcano was now falling so thickly it was almost blinding.

'We go!' Pancho screamed, tottering under the weight of his pack. 'We leave now!'

Lava streamed down the volcano towards the hidden valley as Pancho hurried his heavily laden prisoners and men away from the city. They rushed past the hidden houses, clambered up the secret pathway and into the terrible caverns. Arky was amazed that the tunnel had not collapsed and nothing inside had changed. It was only when they reached the area where the bat colonies had been that Arky realised the animals had not returned. They had somehow known the quake was coming and abandoned the dangerous tunnels. Although he was scared, Arky was glad he didn't have to dodge bat poo again.

Arky was even happier when they emerged from the tunnels. Exhausted by the weights they carried, he and Bear fell to the ground beside the big stone heads. Pancho allowed everyone to rest before they set off down the track of flowers. Arky couldn't help staring at his one-time friend with deep anger, mixed with sadness. *So this is how it feels to be betrayed*, he thought, as a sense of outrage tightened his throat and brought tears to his eyes.

'It is the worst of feelings,' Alice said, reading Arky's face. 'Betrayal is unforgivable.'

'What happens now?' Bear asked anxiously, also staring at Pancho. 'I'm not stupid. He works for Rulec and doesn't need any ransom money. And we can't escape; they have guns on us all the time. Pancho knows we can handle ourselves all too well.'

Arky's throat tightened. It was true. Rulec wouldn't want them alive to tell any tales, especially not after they'd found the city and the fabled Jade-encrusted King.

'We're safe till we get back to the cars,' Doc said. 'Pancho wants us to carry the gold till then. Don't give up hope.'

❖

Amazingly, the volcano remained quiet during their return trip. They clambered along the steep part of the track untroubled and they were lowered, gold and all, safely down the cliff to the jungle floor.

Domingo, Squinty and Scarface were still tied to the tree in the jungle and were very grateful to see everyone. After giving them some food, Pancho joyfully lightened the weight his men carried and loaded the three bandits with heavy packs.

Eventually, after a hard climb up the ravine, they returned to the truck parked in the jungle. Pancho's men loaded the truck with the gold and treasure.

Alice, Doc and the children were marched to one side with Skull-head keeping his gun on them. Suarez and his men were trussed up in the jungle at the top of the ravine.

'I'm giving you more of a chance than you gave my men,' Pancho said to Suarez, as he left them to the mercy of wild animals and the weather.

'You want me to pop this lot now?' Skull-head asked, waving his gun at Doc. 'The boss said they weren't allowed to leave the lost city. We've already disobeyed, even though they carried a lot of treasure. But they've done their job now.'

Mia burst into tears. Alice pulled Arky, Bear and Mia to her, holding them tightly. She jutted her chin out and stared defiantly at Pancho. Doc stepped in front of Alice. 'Kill us, but not the children,' he said. Arky thought his heart would burst with fright, but if his parents could face these men down then so could he. He summoned up all his outrage and glared at Skull-head.

Pancho stepped towards Skull-head. 'I've changed the plan,' he said. He smiled oddly at his brave prisoners. 'You saved my life. I may not be a good person but I do not kill children and women. We will keep you prisoner until we have finished raiding the lost city.'

Arky could barely believe his ears. Pancho was not going to kill them. The colour came back to his face as Pancho bundled them into the rear of the truck along with his gold and locked the door. Pancho's henchmen leapt into the waiting cars and drove away.

Three Little Monkeys

After bumping along roads for hours without stop, Arky fell asleep on a pillow of gold. When Doc shook him awake, the truck had stopped. Men were talking outside. 'We have arrived,' Doc said, checking his watch. 'It's 10 p.m. I wonder where we are?'

'Time to get out,' Pancho called, opening the doors. Arky and Bear stumbled to their feet and clambered out with the others. They found themselves inside a large garage with double electric doors. Pancho, handgun raised, led them from the garage, across a lawn and up the front stairs of a big, brightly lit modern house.

An armed man, who was obviously expecting them, opened the front door. 'I have everything ready.' He smiled at Pancho as Arky followed his parents inside.

'We will sleep here tonight,' Pancho said, as he ushered his prisoners through a lounge room.

Arky noticed the house was dripping with antiques and fine artwork.

'We are all very tired from our long trek. In the morning I will have to go away for a few weeks with my men and return to the lost city to get the rest of the gold. You will be left here as my guests.' Pancho took them down a long hall, through the kitchen to the back of the house, stopping in front of a large door. 'This is the storeroom,' he said, unlocking a solid metal door with a key and then punching a pin into an alarm. 'This room is alarmed. Until recently, it kept treasures away from prying eyes.'

'Who are you?' Doc asked.

'Call me a trader of fine artwork. Many objects come to me from various criminals and I find them good homes.' Pancho opened the door.

Arky peered inside—there was a ramp leading down into a sunken dungeon. Pancho pushed them in and accompanied them into their jail.

Pancho must have rung ahead and got the room ready for their stay. There were mattresses, blankets, several chairs, a table and books, cards, a TV and DVDs jammed into the room, as well as tins of food, cartons of bottled water and a large portable loo in one corner. 'It will be more comfortable than camping, but not the Hilton,' Pancho said, 'and if you are not greedy you will find enough food for a month.' He bowed to Alice. 'So, my friends, I say goodbye.'

'How did you find me at the Sacred Well?' Doc placed a hand on Pancho's shoulder, restraining him for a moment. 'I thought you were from the museum. How come you were diving with me?'

'My boss organised it.' Pancho smiled. 'He has contacts in the museum and paid someone to forge my papers. I sent a friend of mine to visit the archaeologist you were expecting and persuade him to have a long holiday. My job was to steal the Spanish Diary and stop you from getting the Jade-encrusted King.'

'How did your boss know about it?' Arky asked. 'We didn't even know about my dad's plans till we got to the Sacred Well.'

'You might want to tell your stepfather to sack everyone when you get safely home,' Pancho said, patting Bear's head. 'Because someone is a spy. My boss was very excited about the Jade-encrusted King and wanted it for his private museum. He obviously has a grudge against you, Doctor Steele, because his orders were to make you and your family disappear.'

'Rulec!' Bear cried, outraged. 'He wanted us dead. He hates my stepfather. It can only be him!'

'I trusted you.' Doc shook his head sadly. 'I can't believe you would do this, Pancho. And work for Rulec? Unbelievable!'

'You trusted me enough to organise the trek,' Pancho replied, his voice caustic, 'but not enough to share your information. But I knew that, once you thought we were friends, you would tell me more and I would find out where you had hidden the Spanish Diary.

'Unfortunately, Suarez ruined everything by kidnapping us at the well. You should be grateful to him. You would be dead now if Suarez hadn't intervened. Your family rescued me several times and I am alive because of your help. I am a man who repays favours.'

'So, you don't really like Rulec . . .' Arky said. 'And if you take the gold from the city, you won't need to work for him again.'

'You are a very clever young man,' Pancho said. 'I don't plan to start my new life with the death of innocent people on my hands.' He looked at his watch. 'I'd like to stay and chat, but it is time to say goodbye. I will call the police when I am long gone.'

'Well,' Doc sighed, as Pancho slammed and locked the door behind him, 'we are alive and should be thankful.'

'And when we get out,' Arky said, trying to make his dad feel better, 'the ruins will still be there. It is an amazing find.'

'The police might even be able to track down the stolen treasures,' Alice added.

Bear was studying the DVDs. 'We won't be too uncomfortable. It looks like Pancho has supplied us with loads of good movies.'

But Arky didn't want to play cards and watch TV for a month. He wandered around the room, inspecting it closely. It was large and the roof was very high. The floor was cement. The walls were brick but the roof had an air-conditioning vent. It was a small vent and it was blowing air into the room.

'Could we get out through there?' he asked, pointing.

Doc and Alice looked up. 'It's small,' Alice said.

'How would we get up to look?' Bear asked. 'If we stood on the table we'd still be too far below.'

'A child might fit.' Arky studied the vent.

'If Doc stood on the table,' Mia said, 'and Alice stood on his shoulders, and Arky climbed up on Alice and I climbed up on Arky, I might be able to pull the vent cover off and look inside.'

'Worth a try.' Doc smiled. 'Then we could see how big the pipes were and *if* you could crawl inside. Who knows, after the bandits go tomorrow, we might be able to get into another room, find a phone and ring for help.'

Minutes later, Mia was wobbling on Arky's shoulders. Arky's ankles were being firmly held by his mother. Doc was groaning with their weight and the table was managing to stay in one piece.

Bear held his breath, tensely watching the terrible balancing act, as Mia grabbed the vent and pulled with all her might. The vent gave way in a shower of dust and Mia teetered dangerously, almost falling. Wobbling and waving her arms, she regained her balance. Arky grunted with the strain as Mia reached up, grabbed the rim of the vent, pulled herself inside and slithered out of sight.

'She shouldn't have done that!' Doc cried.

Arky clambered down to the ground and Alice jumped down beside him. Doc, rubbing his shoulders, climbed down from the table and they waited as Mia scuffled along the pipe above their heads.

'She can only go one way,' Alice said, looking worried. 'She won't have room to turn. It will be hard to shuffle backwards. What if she gets stuck?'

'Pushing yourself backwards is very hard.' Arky remembered how he had struggled to pull the jade box out of the jaguar statue. 'I hope she'll be okay.'

Minutes ticked by and everyone was getting very worried when the scuffling returned and Mia's head popped into sight. 'It goes along and along . . .' She smiled, her hair filled with spider webs. 'I passed over the men, who are sleeping in a big room. I went to the room that makes the air move. It blows so much air! But nobody was there. There was a vent and I undid it. I wriggled out and I put my hands on a cupboard. I jump down and open a door. I find the garage!'

'We have to try to escape,' Arky said, feeling excited. 'We shouldn't wait.'

'I agree,' Doc said. 'The sooner we get out the better. But how could you get up there with Mia?'

'Mia could you pull me up?' Arky asked.

'No!' Mia's answer was a little cross. 'You are too heavy. But I could tie a small rope to a big bolt that is in here. Then Arky could pull himself up.' She looked at Bear. 'And you might just squeeze through!'

Alice's eyes were big with worry at the thought of the three children disappearing into the dark, but she nodded. 'Three cunning little monkeys might be better than two,' she said. 'You must stick together and help each other—and not take any risks.'

'I think they've proved they can do that,' Doc said, ripping the wires from the TV and video sockets. He tied the cords together and, making their wobbly human ladder once again, Arky managed to get the cords to Mia.

'Good luck,' Alice cried as Arky and Bear climbed up and shuffled after Mia.

The vent was very narrow and pitch-black. Bear was making heavy work of wriggling along the narrow vent in the darkness, puffing loudly behind Arky.

Arky quickly realised the three of them were making too much noise, and he worried they might attract attention. 'Mia,' he whispered. 'You go ahead. Then I will wait five minutes and follow you. Bear, can you wait ten minutes?'

'Horrible idea,' came Bear's reply. 'But yes!'

Mia's scuffling told Arky she had shimmied onwards. Five minutes later, he scrabbled forwards, trying to be as quiet as possible. Like Mia, he passed over a vent that looked down on the sleeping men in a large room. He almost laughed because they had a night-light.

Soon, air blasted into his face. He realised Mia must have got out of the pipes. Then it was his turn to slip out of the air vent, feel for the top of the cupboard and climb out.

Minutes later, Bear joined them in the boiler room and together they crept into the garage beside the truck.

Arky groped around a workbench and found a torch. He clicked it on and studied the garage door. To his dismay, he found it only opened with a remote control. A brief search of the garage showed there were no remotes or inside releases. 'We're trapped,' Arky said, sadness overwhelming him. 'Unless we break down the steel doors, we can't open them.'

'After all we managed to do,' Bear moaned. 'We'll be caught in the garage.'

'I'm not crawling back,' Mia said, wiping her eyes. 'I don't want the bad men to find us!'

Arky realised she was crying. He didn't want to let her down. He had to think of another way to escape. He glanced around, hoping for another idea, trying to remember anything that might help them. *The garage must have been locked behind us,* he thought, *but when Pancho took us from the truck, no one locked the truck!* 'The only lock is on the garage door!' he said aloud, and a huge smile broke out on his face.

'I don't know why you're smiling,' Bear grumbled.

'The back of the truck isn't locked.' Arky opened the truck and climbed inside near the gold. 'Come on. We escape this way. Let's hope they don't check the inside of the truck in the morning. There is no reason to look, and we can hide in here and get a ride. We can jump out at the lights or something!'

With no better plan, Bear and Mia leapt in beside him and smuggled themselves away.

If Goran Rulec were a dancing man he'd have done a little jig. 'You found it!' His voice went up in excitement as he spoke to his man in Central America on the phone.

'The volcano was erupting. We had to get out fast,' Pancho replied. 'It's not safe to go back. I have to do a lot of organising before I return. I also have to keep my team happy and pay them well. We don't want them talking, not after what they've seen. You'll have to wait a few weeks.'

'And the Jade-encrusted King?' Rulec said, barely listening. 'Was it there?'

'It was,' Pancho said. 'Just as Doctor Steele believed.'

'And I take it we won't hear any more from him.' Rulec scowled, hoping Pancho had done what he was ordered to do.

'Let's put it this way: he's underground with his family,' Pancho replied.

'We'll say no more then.' Rulec smiled. 'I want the king shipped to me by the end of the month!'

'We just got back last night,' Pancho said. 'I can't rush this. It's fragile and you want it in one piece.'

'Yes, yes,' Rulec agreed. 'Spend what you need. I'll pick up the bills. You've done really well. Just let me know how you plan to move it safely.'

He put the phone down and imagined Lord Wright searching helplessly for his stepson and his friends. They would just be another group of foreigners who disappeared without trace after being kidnapped by bandits.

'When the news leaks out that they have disappeared,' he said aloud, 'I will send Wright a big wreath of flowers and my sad condolences.'

Treasures and More Treasures

The grinding of the garage's electric door woke Arky. Mia rubbed her sleepy eyes and ducked as low as possible behind the stacks of gold as Pancho's voice reached them. Then, to Arky's dismay, a key was turned in the truck door, locking it from the outside. 'All safe and sound!' It was Skull-head's voice. Doors slammed, the engine whirred and the truck backed out.

'Good plan, Arky,' Bear said sarcastically. 'How do we leap out now?'

Arky was too worried to answer. After a while, he noticed that the bumpy road became smoother.

'I think we are on bitumen,' he said, and had an idea that might help them. 'Listen for sounds and try to remember them,' he said. 'We might be headed to the city. If we escape it might help if we know where we are.'

With nothing better to do, the trio concentrated on where they were going. The traffic noise increased and Arky counted eighty-five stops, which he assumed were traffic lights and then, at one stop, they heard gulls screaming.

'We are beside the sea,' Bear said.

A few seconds later, they bumped over what appeared to be train tracks and there was the sound of heavy machinery and a ship siren.

The truck slowed, reversed and they heard heavy roller doors being raised. Arky also thought he could smell petrol or diesel. Minutes later the truck stopped, the front doors opened and closed, the roller doors squeaked down and there was silence.

'Now what?' Bear asked. 'We get caught when they unload?'

'Not quite,' Arky said. 'Remember how Skull-head said they got out of the truck through a hatch that led to the driver's cabin? It could still be unlocked.'

Bear quickly pulled at the hatch behind him. It opened. Arky beamed with satisfaction. Cautiously, Bear poked his head out. 'We're in a big warehouse,' he whispered. 'I can't see anyone nearby.'

Taking his chance, Bear wriggled through the hatch and Arky and Mia followed. Carefully, they opened the driver's door and climbed out. They dashed for a large pile of cartons and ducked down.

Seconds later, Skull-head and another man, both holding coffee mugs, appeared and unlocked the rear doors of the truck. They began unloading the treasures from the lost city.

While the criminals were busy, Arky looked around for a way to escape. The warehouse was a huge metal shed without windows. The roller doors they had just come through were shut and the men were too close to them to try and open them. All over the concrete floor lay old paintings, antique furniture and containers stacked in rows or piled chaotically. *At least there are plenty of places to hide*, Arky thought. 'Perhaps there is a door at the back,' he whispered. He indicated for Bear and Mia to follow, and then tiptoed towards the rear of the shed, using a long row of containers as cover.

'This place is full of antiquities,' Bear whispered. 'Pancho must be dealing with all the criminals in Central America.'

'He has!' Mia suddenly stopped beside a partially open carton. She reached in and pulled out a little framed painting and a golden cup. 'These are from my church!' She clutched the cup to her. 'This is the communion cup and this is one of the paintings that used to hang near the altar!' Her voice began to rise in outrage. 'Where are our big paintings? We must find them!'

'Quiet,' Arky hissed, trying to pull Mia away from the containers. 'We can come back later.'

Mia refused. She dug her feet in, pulled out other valuable items and put them on the floor.

Pancho's voice cut short Mia's inspection of the carton. She froze as his footsteps came closer. Arky pulled her and Bear down.

'I said I sorted it,' Pancho's voice floated to them. 'Yes, we are getting a helicopter to take us back.'

Arky peeked between two boxes to see who Pancho was talking to. He was on his mobile phone.

'We'll move the Jade-encrusted King and ship it to you. I'll be supervising the airlift. Don't worry, Mr Rulec, I'll look after it. We'll talk later . . .'

'Boss!' Skull-head's voice came from behind Arky and made Bear jump. 'We've finished unloading. What do you want us to do now?'

'I'll come and check it.' Pancho's footsteps faded as he walked away.

Arky wasted no time and hurried Bear and Mia in the opposite direction. When they reached the end of the shed they found a door. Arky opened it carefully and peeked inside. 'An office,' he said. 'No way out, but no one is inside. There's no phone, only a computer.'

'Is it online?' Bear asked, slipping inside. 'If it is, we can send an email to my stepfather and he'll get it on his phone.'

He opened the computer, breathing a sigh of relief. The internet was connected. He quickly accessed his email account and typed as fast as he could: 'We r in a warehouse full of stolen stuff. We can hear seagulls ship siren + machinery and smell petrol. Help. The warehouse is 1 storey metal walls no windows and big roller doors. No other exit. Arky and Mia r with me. We r going to try and get out. Help.'

He had just sent the message when Mia said, 'Someone's coming. Get out!'

Bear scurried from the room and hid with Arky and Mia behind a container, just as Pancho returned. He went into his office and immediately noticed the computer screen was lit. 'Who's been at my computer?' he yelled. 'Have you guys been in the office?'

'The men are all with me,' Skull-head shouted back.

'Then we have intruders!' Pancho roared. 'Search the building! Lock the doors.'

'We're stuffed,' Bear said, looking at Arky. 'What'll we do?

'Hide!' Arky bent down and ran. Bear and Mia hurried after him, listening for the footsteps of hunting men.

Instinctively, Arky kept moving, ducking low behind the containers. 'I think we should separate,' he said when they stopped. 'If one of us is caught, we can try to make them believe we are on our own and one of us might still escape.'

Bear nodded in agreement, but Mia held on to Bear's arm. 'I don't want to be on my own,' she said. 'I will stay with you.'

They had no more time to discuss the idea because the sound of footsteps came closer. Arky peered around a dusty crate. 'Four of them are coming,' he whispered. 'Run!'

Arky ran towards the roller doors and Mia and Bear dashed to the other side. Arky swung to his left along a line of crates and almost ran headfirst into one of the men. There was no hiding now. His first instinct was to turn and run the other way, but he knew he'd be too easily caught. Instead, he stopped, holding his ground. He held his hands high as if he was giving up.

The man walked up to him confidently. 'Got one!' he called, reaching out for Arky.

Arky waited till the last second then, risking all, leapt high and aimed a good kick at the man's groin.

The man went down like a sack of potatoes, groaning in agony. Arky took off, knocking boxes flying, attracting attention away from Mia and Bear. Two more thugs bounded towards him.

Arky was finally trapped near a wall. On one side of him was a stack of containers almost piled to the roof. Seeing a chance, he sprang to the top of a box, hauled himself up higher and stumbled along the top of the row, out of the reach of the two men.

'It's Arky!' Pancho cried, coming up on the other side of the row. 'How did he get here?'

The two men Arky had outfoxed clambered up behind him.

At the end of the row Arky jumped down and, with Pancho only a step or so behind, ran for his life. The two thugs jumped after him and gave chase. Arky ducked and wove, but was finally cornered in a dead-end between large crates.

Menacingly, Pancho stepped forwards, grabbing Arky and lifting him from the ground. 'How did you get here?' he shouted, his breath full of garlic.

Before Arky could answer a groan and scream came from behind.

Mia had clambered up onto a box behind one of the thugs and—using her precious communion cup—had belted the man over the head. Groaning, her victim collapsed onto the concrete. Bear, holding a large metal urn, rammed it over the other man's head. The vase stuck firmly and the man struggled blindly.

Bear then launched himself at Pancho, who was still holding Arky. The three toppled into a screaming, struggling heap, as Bear and Arky battled to escape.

Skull-head arrived and hauled Bear away from Pancho, pinning him against a wall. Mia, cup still in hand, raced up behind Skull-head and began beating him with her weapon. It was to no avail. The other bandits quickly recovered and pinioned her, as well as Arky.

'Are your parents here?' Pancho roared, shaking Arky. 'Tell me or I'll wring your neck!'

BOOM!

The roller doors exploded. Daylight flooded in as hand grenades hit the warehouse floor. Clouds of eye-watering gas filled the room as a troop of heavily-armed men charged into the building.

Arky began coughing and Bear and Mia were spluttering beside him. Then they were scooped up by strong arms and rushed out of the building.

Just Deserts

As Arky gulped at the fresh air and a kind nurse poured saline into Mia's reddened eyes, Lord Wright appeared beside Bear. 'Well done!' he said, grabbing Bear's hand and shaking it.

'How did you find us so fast?' Bear wiped his sleeve past his running nose.

'Lieutenant Gatto rang me when you were kidnapped. Your mother dropped everything and we flew straight here,' Lord Wright said.

'Mum dropped everything?' asked Bear, surprised.

'She was between films,' Lord Wright replied. 'We hired private detectives to keep an eye on warehouses and, on Lieutenant Gatto's advice, we narrowed our choice down to a few warehouses that seemed suspicious.' Lord Wright pointed to an oil depot a few hundred metres away. 'We had private detectives watching this place and they had just sent us a report that a truck had arrived. Then your email came to my phone. That sent us scurrying and I had a rescue team ready in minutes.'

'You can't trust the police,' Arky warned, lowering his voice. 'Lieutenant Gatto is working for Suarez.'

'Not quite right.' Lord Wright smiled. 'Gatto was already very concerned about the fact Suarez was always one step ahead. When you were kidnapped he thought Corporal Topi may be worth watching, so we bugged his phone. Sure enough, we discovered he was leaving messages for Suarez.'

'Pancho left Suarez in the jungle,' Arky said, as Pancho and Skull-head, handcuffed and under guard, were marched into a paddy wagon. 'He's locked Mum and Dad in a house somewhere and he's not an archaeologist.' Arky was relieved to finally tell someone all about it.

'And there's a spy in our house,' Bear blurted out. 'Pancho works for Rulec and he told us that's how he knew about the Spanish Diary!'

'The police will rescue your parents, Arky,' Lord Wright said, 'and we discovered Pancho was not who he appeared to be when Gatto spoke to the museum.' A chauffer-driven car pulled up and Lord Wright signalled it. 'Bear, your mother is anxiously waiting for you. I think it is time I took you all away from here and you got some rest.' He turned to Mia, 'Camilla is also waiting for you.'

That night, when everyone was reunited in Lord Wright's hotel suite, Bear's mum, Linda, listened spellbound to the terrible adventures. Alice and Doc were cuddled up in a pile of big cushions with Arky beside them. Mia was happily sitting on her mother's knee, enjoying a bowl of ice-cream. Bear was eyeing off a pile of delicious desserts on the table, trying to decide which one to choose. Arky had just picked up the biggest banana split, when Lieutenant Gatto arrived to tell them the latest news.

'Suarez and his men have been found alive, but not so well,' he informed them. 'Doctor Steele, your description of the road led us straight to them. He and his men were there and covered with mosquitoes. Suarez was actually happy to see us.' He chuckled and Arky imagined Suarez's relieved face when the police arrived. 'We have charged him and his men with more crimes than I can count. Pancho and his henchmen are charged with kidnapping, theft and dealing in illegal artefacts.'

'And Rulec?' Arky asked. 'Can you do anything about him?'

'Unfortunately, no,' Gatto said. 'Pancho won't tell the police who he was working for, and there are no real leads from him to this Goran Rulec.'

'But we know Rulec tried to steal the Jade-encrusted King!' Arky said, feeling frustrated. 'Pancho told us and he said Rulec wanted us dead!'

'Sadly that is only hearsay,' Doc said. 'It doesn't count in law because it is something Pancho told us, but we can't prove it. The police cannot act unless they have real evidence or proof.'

Gatto smiled at Arky. 'Pancho won't talk. But all is not lost. We have alerted the international police to our suspicions. I suspect your Goran Rulec will have to be very careful from now on. International artefact theft is a very serious crime.'

'We found our church's treasures in the warehouse,' Mia said. 'Will they be returned?'

'We are going through all the stolen things now,' Gatto said. 'It will take us years to find many of the owners, but you and your mother can come with me tomorrow and, when we locate your church's treasures, we will let you take them back to your village.'

Ten days later, with reports that the volcano had stopped erupting, Doc flew out for the hidden city along with a team of experts and archaeologists.

That same day, Bear and Arky, along with Alice, Linda and Lord Wright were flown in Lord Wright's private helicopter to Mia's hometown. They had been invited to be special guests at the first church service held in the town for several months. Mia and Camilla had gone home the day before to help plan the special celebration.

The fact that Linda was coming too made Mia jump up and down with excitement. 'A real film star,' she gushed. 'A famous lady coming to my village. Everyone will be so jealous that I know her!'

The helicopter landed in a field just outside of a small town with a large brick seventeenth-century church standing on a hill. The town mayor shook Arky's hand the moment he stepped off the helicopter and the town band played so loudly and enthusiastically it drowned out the sound of the helicopter's blades.

A fine black car drove them through the streets, which were filled with posters of Bear's mother in her last film. People waved joyfully as they passed by.

'They're very excited,' Arky said. 'I can't believe they have gone to so much trouble just for a church service.'

'It means we'll have to listen to long, boring speeches,' Bear said. 'It looks like it's been a long time since the mayor has had the chance to be so important.'

'Don't be so rude,' Alice said. 'There is more to today than just speeches.'

'Your stepfather has organised a special gift for the church,' Linda added, waving like a queen to the waiting crowds lining the streets, 'so you can try to be polite.'

She had no more time to explain about the gift, because the car stopped outside the church and Bear and Arky were led inside as bells tolled loudly in welcome.

The town's new young priest, decked out in brilliant robes, stood by the altar. People crowded into every spare seat. The church was stunning, with old religious paintings, icons, gold offerings, beautiful woodwork and sumptuous tapestries. Arky understood why tourists would visit the church and why the town had suffered so badly after the theft of all the artworks.

Arky and Bear were shown to a front seat with Mia and Camilla. The priest started the service.

'How beautiful is my church now,' Mia whispered, during a hymn. 'Everyone is so happy with our new priest. Hear how well he sings.'

Arky noticed Mia's ears went bright red when the priest offered everyone communion from a very battered golden cup. Afterwards the mayor gave a big speech. Bear and Arky wriggled uncomfortably as every word was in Spanish and it went forever. At one stage, everyone stared at Arky and Bear, and started clapping. Arky guessed the mayor was thanking them for the return of all the church treasures.

Finally, Lord Wright stepped forwards with a beautifully wrapped box. He handed it to the priest. The priest unwrapped a wonderful new golden communion cup and held it high for everyone to admire. Then he picked up the old cup that Mia had dented in her attack on the bandits and placed it high on the altar.

'The cup is going to be an icon now,' Camilla explained. 'It will not be used again, but the story of how children saved this village will be told for one hundred years!'

Mia blushed. 'I thought I was in trouble for denting the cup,' she said. 'But now I am important. It feels funny to be important.'

The mayor called the children forwards. Everyone cheered. To Arky's shock, they were hugged warmly by the mayor as Lord Wright told the village he had one more surprise.

'I have sponsored a small museum,' he said. 'It will be built next year and it will display many artefacts found in the hidden city. It will bring tourists and more work for your village.'

Mia and Camilla stared at Lord Wright in astonishment.

'How wonderful!' Camilla hugged Lord Wright, Linda, Alice and the boys.

Mia gave Arky a hug. Then she grabbed Bear and, laughing, gave him a huge kiss.

A camera flashed to record the moment.

Arky and Bear returned home the next day and went back to school. The following school holidays Alice and Linda collected them and they flew back to Central America. They had been invited to the opening of the Lost City and the removal of the Jade-encrusted King to the capital museum.

In Lord Wright's helicopter they flew over the jungle, past the twin-eyed volcano that simmered against the sky. Linda was dressed up for the cameras and Alice was looking beautiful in a smart suit and new shoes. The boys were also decked out in fancy clothes.

The helicopter circled the hidden city. Arky looked down. The city, not lost any more, was like a beehive, with people scurrying everywhere. Crates and tents, plastic bags, spades and shovels littered the streets.

The helicopter landed in the playing court. Arky noticed the court had been cleared and the skulls were gone. Everywhere they looked, people were photographing every building, collecting and protecting every pot, mask, skull and artefact. Officials and important visitors were being guided through the ruins. Doc met them as they landed and took them straight to the palace. Scaffolding, holding the tottering walls in place, surrounded the building. The ash had been cleared and the Jade-encrusted King had been found in one piece, despite the damage the volcanic eruption had caused to the palace.

With Doc accompanying them, the boys were allowed to enter the chamber where King Huemac now lay in a huge glass coffin ready for his trip to the city museum in a military helicopter.

Every now and then, Linda gathered up Bear, while she posed for photos. Doc, Lord Wright, Arky and Alice were largely ignored. 'It is a curse, I think,' Alice said, watching Linda pose for photo after photo. 'She can't go anywhere without cameras in her face.'

'Everyone will think she found the city.' Arky laughed, as Bear pulled faces at the cameras and ruined a few shots. Arky knew his friend was desperate to escape.

'But everyone will read about her being here,' Doc said, coming up behind them. 'People aren't that interested in archaeology. A famous actress is a selling point. When it opens for tourists, many people will want to come to the city because they will have read about her adventures.'

Doc led Bear and Arky up the stairs of the pyramid of the sun. It was time for the Jade-encrusted King to be removed. Arky noticed the stairs were covered in dark brown marks. He assumed the marks were bloodstains left by the hundreds of victims sacrificed with the sorcerer's knife.

At the top of the pyramid he was surprised to find seats waiting for them, and there was a wonderful view over the city.

The volcano gave a big burp and Arky wondered if it had belched like that when Alfonso Pezaro and Francisco were there. He imagined that the Spanish conquistadors would have sat where he and Bear sat now. Pezaro and Francisco would have been honoured guests before a crowd waiting in fear for the first sacrifices to start. He pictured how the people would have watched as the evil sorcerer began his work.

But Arky was glad that today, instead of a sorcerer cutting out hearts to impress the crowds and to try to bring King Huemac back to life, modern magic was going to make the legend come true. The great King Huemac was being brought back to life through television and he was going to fly.

❖

Goran Rulec waited by his phone for Pancho to ring about the Jade-encrusted King. As the days wore on, he became suspicious. His usual sources could give him no information, which made him think Pancho may have met with foul play or perhaps died in the jungle. At the back of his mind he wondered if Pancho might have stolen all the treasures for himself. He became more worried by the week.

He used a special phone that diverted and re-routed his number, so he couldn't be traced, and rang Pancho's phone many times. No one answered.

When his spy in Lord Wright's house was sacked, he knew something was really wrong. Finally, he sent one of his most trusted men to find out what had happened. The man flew out to Central America and tried to hunt Pancho down. Eventually, Rulec discovered Pancho had been arrested and one of his spies told him the full story. Angry, Rulec realised he wouldn't ever be able to get to the city and steal the Jade-encrusted King.

Several months later, Rulec watched his hated enemy Lord Wright on television. Lord Wright stood atop a stone pyramid with his beautiful wife and her brat, Belvedere. Behind him were Doctor Steele and his wife, the famous mountaineer, and their son.

Rulec's face reddened with anger as a close-up revealed the magnificent jade and gold mummy to to the world for the first time. And then the fabled King Huemac was lifted into a helicopter.

Furious, Rulec picked up an expensive vase and threw it at Lord Wright and the TV.

Then he went down to his private museum and stared long and hard at the empty space where the Jade-encrusted King should have been lying in pride of place.

'Next time,' he brooded, '—and there will be a next time—I will not trust idiots. I will go myself and get my revenge on Lord Wright and the Steeles.'